MW00966440

The
Final Solution
to the
Irish Question?

by Rick Spier

To Jane & Thad
With LOVE.

Rick Spier

Published in 2016 by Moon Donkey Press, LLC
Clyde Hill, WA USA

First Edition

Library of Congress Control Number: 2016917181

ISBN: 978-0-9754398-4-5

Cover by Anú Design
Collierstown, Tara, County Meath, Ireland

Printed by Worzalla Publishing Company
Stevens Point, WI USA

Moon Donkey Press, LLC

Also by Rick Spier

O'Sullivan's Odyssey

*The Legend of Shane the Piper:
A Novel Memoir*

The Courage of His Convictions

For Butch and Daddy

The
Final Solution
to the
Irish Question?

IT WAS SOMETHING HE WOULD NEVER TIRE OF, watching the rain, that is, not after his childhood spent in a place where it almost never came and the glare and the heat and the dust so burdened his Northern constitution. He loved to go for long evening walks in it, letting it soak him to the bone in defiance of the reproof of passers-by, to feel it thumping his hat and stinging his face and running down his shirt, its coolness soothing in equal measure to his skin and his soul. Afterward, he would strip his sodden clothes onto the bathroom floor and stand naked before the mirror as he combed the water from his long, thick black hair and bushy beard. Then he would wrap himself in a terry robe and repair to his recliner by the front window, lie back, let his mind go blank and just stare at the drops flickering through the light of the street lamp until the mesmerizing constancy lulled him into a deep and easy sleep. The heavens were bountiful in this northern city, too, and the rain came often, so that he frequently awoke with the light of dawn peeking through his window after another restful night in his chair.

"Little slices of Heaven," he called those evenings, knowing as he did that he would always remember them as the best part of his life.

But he wasn't sitting as he watched the rain tonight, and his mind was alert and receptive, for this night was one he'd long anticipated, one for which he'd planned and trained ever since he was a little boy. Everything was finally set now, and soon he would live in a new place, under a new name and with a new guise, a new history and new, pleasant-albeit-trivial work to occupy his time. But while he was eager to get on with it, he couldn't help lingering for this last evocative look, to savor these last triumphal moments.

His thoughts turned philosophical as he watched the raindrops fragment on the street and disappear into anonymous rivulets that vanished inexorably down the storm drain, and it occurred to him that a drop of rain was very much like a person, each individual unique and complete in itself though blending ultimately into an indistinct mass hurtling toward a destiny at once unknown and unknowable, an ending as sudden as it was inescapable and final, and a vanishing as utter as if it had never been, its entire lifespan but a blink of Nature's eye.

"One death is a tragedy," he thought, "but a million is a statistic." Could there be a more perfect metaphor for it than raindrops?

Turning from the window, he left his living area and went into his studio to set the failsafe timer and take a last loving look at his masterpiece. Circling his spotlit workbench to admire his handiwork, he saw in each exquisite detail the culmination of his life's work, the denouement of his ten-year apprenticeship, ten plodding, anonymous years spent in glum, tribal Belfast producing the essays in his craft—his works of art, his many sculptural impressions of *Bríd*, the Fire Goddess, all rendered in precious metals over bronze and arising phoenix-like from her own living flame, a lithe, willowy nude dancing in sensual, writhing arabesques ornamented with music and poetry made visible—as he slowly, carefully, secretively collected the metals more precious and rare needed to construct this, his *magnum opus*.

He smiled again, allowing himself a moment of shameless

pride, though it faded when his eyes fell upon the figure's face. Unlike his previous pieces, this one bore the chaste likeness of his mother as she held his little sister in her arms, her serene countenance rendered in exacting photographic detail as she'd been in that last moment of her existence, as she was still in his memory. He'd saved her especially for now so that she could be the *phoenix* of his revenge, and when she arose in flame, she would sweep away eight centuries of injustice and his vengeance would be personal and visceral and magnified thousands of times over by the chagrin of the Orangemen seeing Ireland united in their despite. He would savor it all from afar, too, triumphant in the knowledge that he would live out his natural life in comfort and safety.

As he stared into his mother's hypnotic gaze, however, his mind began suddenly to spin and, before he could stop it, reality collapsed into hallucination and he was lost to himself, transported back to that terrible moment when the bomb exploded, watching as the fireball engulfed his mother and sister, feeling himself lifted, flying through the air, striking his head ...

Then it was gone as quickly as it came and he was leaning heavily on the workbench, his heart racing and his nerves electric from the rush of cortisol and adrenaline.

It had been a long time since he had a flashback, and what caused this one, he couldn't tell. He wasn't stressed, after all, but buoyant and happy. And why was the imagery so different this time? Whereas in the past, his mother's haunting eyes were locked upon him in stern expectation, as she pointed a demanding finger and exclaimed, "I want you to avenge us!", here her eyes were closed and her head bowed as she prayed fervently to God to forgive her of her trespasses as she forgave those who trespassed against her. What did it mean? Was it a visitation of her spirit meant to test of his resolve? If so, why *now* when his work was almost done?

But then logic reminded him that flashbacks were merely illusions sprung of misfiring synapses and chemical imbalances in his injured brain, and certainly there were no such things as spirits. Life was random and things happened for no reason whatsoever and survival went to the fittest and/or the luckiest and the only reality was the *here* and the *now* that his five senses conveyed to him! And yet, in the absence of the supernatural, this vision of his mother praying for forgiveness and to be herself forgiving could only come from something within himself, and that thing must be, could only be ...

Doubt!

The thought shocked and frightened him.

Doubt?

Was there *doubt* within his heart that clamored for notice that he would never give because he was willfully blindered to all but the road ahead, *doubt* about whether it was the *right* road because he took it as a little boy and then followed mindlessly in the footsteps he lay before himself, never pausing to examine their rationality with a mature, experienced man's reasoning?

His eyes wandered again to his mother's, and as the flashback imagery played over in his mind, the feeling grew within him that it wasn't so much a vision as a *memory*, perhaps from a life he'd lived in a time long ago and a place far away, although one incomplete and lacking its original context, without which he could divine no meaning. But should he take a rational step back and reflect on it, he wondered, or was he just allowing ephemera to obfuscate his purpose?

As *doubt* piled upon *doubt* and his agitated mind whirled with questions, what felt concrete suddenly seemed less so, and once again he felt himself slipping away, saw the image of his praying mother begin to form, felt his heart racing and his muscles tensing ...

But this time he intercepted it and subsumed the fear and

helplessness into his rage, his rage that had always kept him grounded and moving forward, his righteous rage for all that had been stolen from him, his rage at *himself* for allowing this moment of weakness! Turning it outward, he slammed his fists on the workbench, shrieked "***FUCK!***" with such violence that it rang in his ears and stalked from his studio without a backward glance.

Slamming the door, he strode angrily into his bathroom, where he leaned over his lavatory and took a long, searching look in the mirror, probing his unblinking eyes as if trying to delve into the deepest abyss of his soul. What he found there and whether he liked it or not, he gave no clue, for no emotion colored his mien before he suddenly sprang into action.

Removing his tweed cap, he pulled away the band that bound his hair into a ponytail, assessed the inch-long white roots that came from leaving it undyed for a month, then butched it to a clean-cut, homogeneously white half-inch length with electric shears. Next, he buzzed his beard to stubble, smoothed his face with a razor and removed the hazel contacts that masked his brilliant blue eyes, then showered, dressed and donned a pair of heavy black-rimmed eyeglasses. As he performed his methodical ablutions, his inner turmoil receded and he felt sanguine again, his psyche soothed by returning to the swaddling womb of his circumscribed path and the act of taking the next blindered step upon it.

Standing before the mirror, he looked himself up and down appraisingly, then turned away, satisfied that no one would recognize him as the man he'd been but moments before, especially when he dropped his faux Ulster accent and spoke his native American English. Going to the back door, he put on his raincoat and a Yankees baseball cap, grabbed his packed duffle bag and exited into the alley, where he strapped the luggage to his bicycle, mounted and, without a backward glance, rode quickly away.

THE REVEREND DOCTOR Ian Patrick MacDonnell Th.D.—
or "just plain Pat," as he presented himself to the world—stood
by the window of the stern observation deck and watched as
the lights of Belfast disappeared behind a curtain of rain,
thinking that this late-night ferry voyage to Stranraer in rough
seas would be the perfect ending to a perfectly lousy day, and a
perfectly lousy trip, for that matter, one he wasn't all that
happy about taking in the first place. For he hated South
Armagh with a particular passion, hated everything about it,
the people, the culture, the violence, the people, the fanaticism,
the atavism, the people, the sights, the smells, the people …
Hell, he even hated the hatred that so defined the place,
because, after so many years of being the most militarized
region in all of Western Europe, even the very air was thick
with it! It was echoed even in the name of his village, Ballyvoo,
a corruption of the Irish *Baile Fhuath*, "the Place of Hatred," so-
called because it had been the scene of an ancient battle
between two clans so fiercely and mutually inimical that, after
they slaughtered each other to a man, their women and
children took up arms and continued the butchery. The blood
they spilled might well have impregnated the earth with their
hatred, for animosity continued to plague local residents right
down through the centuries, changing its form and finding new
objects from time to time, but forever cursing the killing field
that was Ballyvoo.

The enmity of present times dated from the Plantation of
Ulster in 1607, when English-speaking Protestants (mostly
Presbyterians from Scotland and Anglicans from northern
England) were transplanted to the north of Ireland and settled
on lands seized from rebellious Gaelic lords. From that time
onward, the North of Ireland was the contentious abode of two

sectarian tribes so fiercely and mutually inimical that they'd been at each other's throats for nearly four centuries, even though the differences between them were so superficial as to border on the absurd. The Protestants (Orange) hated the Catholics (Green) and the Catholics hated the Protestants, the Unionists hated the Nationalists and vice versa, thank you very much, while the poor befuddled British soldiers hated them all for bringing them into harm's way in the first place. Then there was the even more nebulous stuff—Anglophilic vs. Gaelophilic, Democratic Unionist vs. Sinn Féin, East Belfast vs. West Belfast, Rangers vs. Celtic, No Surrender vs. *Tiocfaidh ár lá*, us vs. them, this vs. that, shit vs. shite—in short, all the atavistic tribal baggage of "the past" that made Northern Ireland the Balkans of the British Isles and proof positive that, in a country with no Africans, Asians, Hispanics, Jews, Muslims or Indians of either sort to hate, White People would *improvise*!

But while Pat MacDonnell hated all that hatred, mostly what he hated about South Armagh—and Ballyvoo, in particular— were the people who lived there, who, not coincidentally, disliked him in equal measure. The reasons for it were many and varied, but they began with the fact that his father, a flaccid and ineffectual sod even in the rare times when he wasn't drunk, gave him that *Proddie* name, "Ian," after some footballer or other to whom he'd taken a shine in his youth and never grew out of it, which, along with the fact that "MacDonnell" could swing either to Orange or Green, gave him the dubious distinction of being universally suspect in both of Northern Ireland's reciprocally hate-mongering communities. Even the Catholic kids who'd known he was one of theirs taunted and bullied him unmercifully as a child, and being the sensitive sort that he was, he often came home with tears streaming down his cheeks and his clothes muddy and askew from their rough treatment, only to receive more of the same and worse from his vicious harpy of a mother.

"Shut yer hole, yeh little faggit," she would scream as she slapped him about the head, "or I'll shut it for yeh, so I will! How I bred sich a spoineless brood o' rannies is beyond me, so it is, what with me martyred fadder bein' corp'ral o' the Ballyvoo Brigade, and himself turnin' in his grave at the very thought o' yez, I've no doubt, so I don't." Then, turning her bile upon Ian's father, "'Tis all yeh're fault, yeh worthless gobshite, and none o' me own, d'yeh hear? An' me slavin' from dawn to dawn, the layin' hen o' this family, so I am, an' this the thanks I get, the loikes of yeh an' them little boadies there to call the men o' me house! *Men*? HA! Why I've more bollix than the bunch o' yeh hand-shandies all put together, so I do!"

Whether she hated her husband more or her children, or just life itself, was never really quite clear to anyone, but her rancor, in any case, was non-discriminatory and her daily ranting began with the rooster and continued long after little Ian and his four elder brothers had slunk off to their room, and sometimes even after his father had slunk off to the local to try to drink up the gumption to come home and kill her, which, fortunately or unfortunately depending upon one's point of view, he never quite managed to do.

Even Ian's brothers tormented him, calling him "Mr. Paisley" after the Orange demagogue who shared his Christian name, an epithet that became so firmly attached to him that even the priest called him so, and right to his very face no less.

So there was just no peace to be had anywhere for little Ian—that is, until he went through a growth spurt and suddenly stood head and shoulders above even the tallest of his nemeses, and, after he'd splattered a nose or two and left gaping gaps in a few grins, word got round that Mr. Paisley had best be left alone. And left alone, he was, too, not that it brought him any peace, mind you, because their whispers, disdainful looks and cold shoulders merely meant that they hated him in silence and from a discrete distance.

16

Not surprisingly, the first thing young Ian did when he felt himself man enough was to leave Ballyvoo without so much as a "good riddance" and slip across the border into the Republic, and the first thing he did after that was to change his name to "Patrick," which—without his permission—the world around him immediately shortened to "Paddy," which, in turn, he hated almost as much as "Ian" because it was one of the many ethnic slurs hurled at Catholics back in Ballyvoo. But, what could you do, and at least as "Paddy" he was no one's punching bag in the Republic and, surely, would never be mistaken for an Orangeman because no self-respecting Proddie would ever allow himself to be called so. Anyway, after taking care of first things first, the first thing he did after making his way to Dublin was to lie about his age so he could join the Irish Police force, *An Garda Síochána na hÉireann* (literally, "The Guardians of the Peace of Ireland").

And that was where the newly-christened *Paddy* MacDonnell hoped to leave the poison and spleen of Ballyvoo behind, because, even with his tormented childhood and adolescence, he remained a sensitive and gentle soul who was sooner moved to empathy and pity, sometimes even for those who were his erstwhile tormentors, and having to restructure their facial features in order to make them leave him alone brought him no pleasure at all. So he wanted to serve those like himself and to protect them from the ruthless and avaricious of the world who would take advantage of their weakness.

But the depth of depravity he found working as a beat cop in the slums of North Dublin sickened him beyond disgust and sowed within him with a soul-devouring disillusionment, for the guilty were so often just so *blatantly* guilty, while the weak whom he hoped to serve and protect were often so culpable in their predicament as to elicit revulsion in him rather than compassion. Gradually, his disappointment turned his salient tenderness into rage and the more he raged, the more the choking hatred that choked his youth bore down upon him, till he could find solace only in alcohol and even then only while he was actually drinking. So he drank all the time, even sneaking nips while on the beat, and the more he drank, the more he hated the world around him, and the more he hated, the more he drank, till life became a vortex spiraling him down into the cesspool of Hell.

Then one day, his ticking time-bomb exploded and he almost killed a man, a petty drug-dealer suspected of raping a thirteen-year-old girl, a repeat offender who'd yet surrendered peacefully and was lying face-down on the sidewalk in token of submission. But after handcuffing him, Paddy turned him over and punched him in the face till his knuckles were torn and bleeding and the man was unrecognizable, not for anything the man was or did, exactly, but just that Paddy was blinded by hatred and wanted to kill him because, in that particular moment, what he really wanted to do was to kill himself.

Unfortunately for Paddy—or, rather, *fortunately* as he would later be the first to admit—a witness caught the whole thing on video, including Paddy fighting with the Gardaí who pulled him off the suspect and him cursing them and shrieking like the banshee herself. When it was revealed that he had a flask of vodka on him and that his blood-alcohol level was well above legal intoxication, the media had a field day and the video was shown repeatedly on RTE, while his picture was plastered on the front of every newspaper on the island with headlines that screamed "POLICE BRUTALITY!" and "GARDA A DRUNKEN THUG!" Of course, Paddy was cashiered from the force unceremoniously and faced multiple charges, which his solicitor, playing on Paddy's difficult past, clean service record and the despicable nature of his victim's crime, was able to plea-bargain down to a year in a rehab facility, with charges to be dropped upon successful completion of the program.

Although he'd been a Guardian of the Peace and there were things he loved about the force, it was ironic that the first real peace Paddy ever knew came to him while he was institutionalized, as the cares and stresses of the world fell away and, with the help of the warm and professional staff and through the process of the program, he gradually began to heal and to find himself becoming whole. He especially came to relish the group counseling sessions, wherein the convalescents exposed their vulnerabilities and thereby assured each other that they weren't alone in their emotional suffering. It gave him a feeling of family, too, and it was in that setting that he learned he had a talent for brainstorming and that he could use it in combination with his rediscovered compassion to help others take a step back from themselves and look dispassionately into their lives and gain an outsider's insight into the problems they faced, and thereby find illumination that had eluded them because they were too blinded by their pain to see it. It was that ability to help people that brought Paddy the greatest peace, and, from it, grew a renewed commitment to and understanding of what he felt to be his avocation in life—helping those who were unable to help themselves. Indeed, it came to him sharply and focused when, near the end of his stay, his psychologist asked, "What do you think you might want to do with your life?"

"I want to help people," he answered simply, knowing in his heart that it was the simple truth.

"No," the woman persisted, leaning forward for emphasis. "That's not what I mean. I'm asking what *you*, Ian Patrick MacDonnell, want to do with *your* life?"

Leaning forward himself and matching her intensity of voice and gaze, Paddy replied, "I want to help those who can't help theirselves, Dr. Ferguson, just like you do."

The woman relaxed then and smiled. "Yes, from all that I've seen, I think that's your true purpose in this life. So, do you want to think about a career in mental health counseling? You'd be very good at it, you know, and I can help you get started."

"Well," he answered hesitantly, "I don't know. I think I should poke about a bit first and see what gets stirred up."

"I see," she said, raising an eyebrow. "You've come a long way from where you started."

"I know. And I'm right proud o' meself for it, too."

When his time was up and with no means of supporting himself and knowing he couldn't stay in Ireland for the notoriety he'd garnered—indeed, the media were crowded round the gates on his day of release—Paddy accepted Dr. Ferguson's offer to arrange a job for him in her home town of Glasgow, all the way across the Irish Sea in Scotland. It wouldn't be much to begin with, she explained, just a volunteer counselor for a local Alcoholics Anonymous, though he could at least "get his feet wet" right away and make connections in the counseling community, while still having time to "poke about."

"Sure, that's grand so, Doctor, and I can see the possibilities, too. But what'll I live on?"

"Well," she replied, and he thought her eyes went a bit coy on him, "that's a bit more dodgy. But I think I have a solution that will benefit the both of us. My father, bless his soul, is all by himself in the house now that Mother has gone, and, with me here in Ireland and his old friends dying faster than he can make new ones, he wants for a bit of company and looking after. So, if you're in agreement, you'll live with him and get your room and board and a bit of pocket money in exchange for some work about the house and keeping an eye on things for me."

Paddy stiffened at that. "I'm not lookin' for charity, Dr. Ferguson, or to be a burden to anyone."

"Oh, it's not charity, Paddy, I can assure you of that. You'll do a fair day's work for your keep, and, besides, if you think you'll be the one who's a burden, then you don't know much about old folks, do you?"

"No, I suppose I don't," he admitted, and as they shared a smile, he took a good look at her as a woman for the first time and noticed that she was quite lovely, if in a scholarly sort of way and with as many years beyond thirty in her as he was shy of it. But there was no inkling of romance in his appraisal; he knew she was too far above him, which, if he'd considered that for a moment, would've told him he'd not come as far as he thought.

"Are we in agreement then, Paddy?"

"We are so. And if it's all the same to yeh, ma'am, I think it'll be just plain 'Pat' from now on."

"Aye, just plain Pat it is then. And my name is Anne, but my friends call me 'Andie' after my father."

The freshly-minted "Pat" left for Glasgow soon after, following in the footsteps of millions of other expatriating Irish by taking the ferry from Dún Laoghaire to Liverpool (a crossing which he devoted entirely to vomiting over the railing), and then taking trains up North from there. It was his first time out of Ireland, of course, and he found the experience of being on his own while going new places and seeing new things and different kinds of people exhilarating and liberating, so much so that, when he reached his destination, he felt an insistent urge to just keep going and follow The Road wherever it led. But he didn't, and, because of what he found in Glasgow, the impulse to go any further never came upon him again.

From Dr. Andie Ferguson's rather vague description of her father, Pat hadn't really known what to expect. But when he arrived (and much to his relief, if the truth be told), he found Dr. Andrew Ferguson to be the paragon of all the things a man should aspire to in his advancing age. That is, his bit of garden was lush and well-tended, his small house neat, tidy and homey, and he, himself, trim, well-groomed, firm of hand, sound of mind and with a welcoming smile warming his intelligent and distinguished features, all of which gave him, in short, the air of a man who'd lived his life well, if simply perhaps, and was more than content to let that be his epitaph.

"Come in with you, now laddie," he fairly boomed as he drew Pat inside. "My Andie has told me so much about you and 'tis both honored and pleased I am to have you in my home. Or "our" home, as I should say, since it's to be yours, too, and for as long as you want."

"Thank yeh, Dr. Ferguson, and the honor and pleasure are me own. I'd like to say the same o' you, sir, but, to be honest, Andie's told me next to nothin' about yeh. Come to think of it, I don't even know what kind of a doctor yeh are. Are yeh a psychologist, too?"

"Nae, laddie," Ferguson replied in his cultured burr. "I'm no physic of the mind or body. I'm a *Doctor Theologiae*, which is a doctor of the soul, if you take my meaning—a *minister*."

Pat couldn't help but be taken aback at that, and he finally understood Andie's coyness (or so he thought, anyway) in broaching the subject of him living with her father, for she was well aware that if she'd told him the man was a minister, he'd have declined the offer on the spot, no matter what incentive she might proffer. In fact, religion was a sore subject with him, the erstwhile "Mr. Paisley" whose Catholic "Father" and church "family" had contributed to, rather than assuaging, his childhood suffering. Indeed, it was something he talked about more than once in their sessions, telling of how all the clerics in Ballyvoo—Catholic and Protestant alike—had been such dour and forbidding old begrudgers, as black in countenance as the cloth they wore, men who preached in strident tones of a jealous and vengeful God, one who smote his enemies and damned his transgressors to eternal torment, with always the hint (and usually more) that those miscreants were to be found just across the village in that *false* temple worshipping the false god of the apostate, doing far more with their sectarian chauvinism and firebrand rhetoric to keep hatred alive in Ballyvoo than to bring about Christian reconciliation and healing.

And yet, as Pat took in this smiling and happy person so jovially welcoming him into his home, the incongruity with his former experience of "faith" could not have been more stark, so much so, in fact, that even the thought of it was swept from his mind by the man's warmth and congeniality.

"I'll tell you straight away, now," Ferguson said, after they'd dispensed with the cordialities and settled comfortably into overstuffed chairs, "that Andie has told me all about your little scrape with Uncle Al, and, just so you know, I don't allow the stuff in my home. Not that I've anything against it in principle, now, mind you, for a dram in the evening with a warm fire and a good book is one of the joys of life, I'd say. It's just that I had my full share of it in my youth, rather as you have yourself, from what I gather."

"Sure, Father … I mean Reverend, or is it somethin' else entirely?"

"It's none of that, lad. Just plain "Andy" will do. I'm a Unitarian minister, if you want to know, and we're pretty informal about things."

"Oh, I see. I can't say as I know much about you fellahs, beyond the fact that yeh weren't kindly thought of by either side back home. But, then, Ballyvoo's like that—nobody likes anybody, especially if they're in any way different from theirselves. Sure, if it hasn't been said o' the place that, if God wanted to give the world an enema, he'd stick the nozzle right smack through the heart of Ballyvoo."

"And here I was thinking that honor had been reserved for Glasgow!" Ferguson rejoined.

After that, their conversation wandered back to Unitarianism, with Ferguson explaining their syncretic approach to faith and that they were united by shared values rather than creed or dogma, because it wasn't what you said or believed that was ultimately important in the world, but what you *did*. And that resonated deeply with Pat, especially coming, as it did, from such a positive and compelling persona as Andy Ferguson. Then the conversation moved further afield as they spoke of many things both personal and in the world about them, becoming so deeply engrossed in each other that they forgot to eat dinner and only remembered to go to bed because they found themselves yawning more than talking.

As he lay in the dark pondering his day and the queer but undeniable feeling that he'd somehow come home, Pat said to himself, "I could stay right here forever, so I could."

After that, things progressed rather quickly for him, as he and Ferguson became fast friends and constant companions, finding each in the other an intellectual and philosophical reflection that was yet just enough askew to keep things interesting. Pat found his work with the A. A. group (which just happened to meet at Ferguson's church) incredibly rewarding, too, as his calling came to him there amid the familiar feeling of interconnectedness that he'd discovered while in rehab, and his ministering to the suffering and their need for healing invigorated him and left him at peace with himself and the world around him like he had never been before, as if he were at home among his family and doing just what he was supposed to be doing. On top of that, he found a family among Ferguson's Unitarians, who represented a patchwork quilt of castes, colors, creeds, races, and ethnicities and celebrated the differences amongst themselves as a strength rather than a source of fear and contention. It wasn't that he "found Jesus," exactly, or experienced any renewal of faith in God or an afterlife, but he did see how those beliefs brought people comfort and hope and he already knew how important those things were in his own ministry. For he'd learned that he couldn't redeem the fallen all in a day and that he must work incrementally to help them find the foundation upon which to build a better life, and that it sometimes just meant helping them to keep themselves alive from day to day, because he realized that the old cliché was yet a fount of truth and that where there was life there could be hope and, if there was hope, then redemption was at least possible.

Then, after attending a service one Sunday and hearing Ferguson speak simply but eloquently on the Golden Rule and seeing how it so resonated with his congregation, Pat found the philosophy which he knew would define him henceforth and saw his path in life open before him.

"I know what I want to do with my life," he told Ferguson over supper that evening.

"Hm? And what's that?"

"I want to be a Unitarian minister."

"Yes, I thought so," the man replied, as dryly as if Pat had said, 'It's raining outside.' "But it's easier said than done, you know, and you'll have to finish your schooling and get a degree."

"I know and I want to do that, too, though I don't know how I'll pay for it yet."

"I'll see to that. I'm a guest lecturer at the University, you know, and I'm sure something can be arranged."

"Thank you for that, Andy. I'll accept yer help gladly, but I insist on payin' ych back."

"Paying me *back*? Och, boy, don't you get it yet? Why do you think Andie sent you here?"

"Andie *sent* me? She didn't … I mean … I thought …"

"She saw a gentle soul with great potential for the good and sent you here so I could help you find your way, and a wise lassie she is for it, too, if you're as lost as all that. We'll help you get your degree and your credentials and you'll pay us back by doing a good turn for someone else someday. It's called the 'circle of life.' Have you never heard of it?"

So with Ferguson's help and mentoring, Pat eventually received his Th.D. from the University of Glasgow, thereby becoming a Doctor, himself, a thing of which he could never have dreamed during his life of darkness in Ballyvoo, and was ordained into the Unitarian ministry. During those years, he continued his work with alcoholics and drug addicts, in the process developing a reputation that spread through the Lowlands and Highlands and even into England and Ulster. He also took on duties at the Unitarian Church, becoming, in practice if not name, Ferguson's assistant minister, and then his replacement when the man retired shortly after Pat's ordination.

But perhaps the most meaningful development in Pat's life was the fact that he'd married Andie a year after coming to Glasgow. Their courtship began during her visit home for that first Christmas after his move. They'd been alone together in the evening and deep in free-flowing conversation, when Pat, realizing he'd been going on about himself and his work, said, "Oh, I'm sorry, Doctor. Here yeh are, off the clock, and me talkin' shop at yeh."

"I'm not your doctor anymore, Pat," she said. "In fact, I've resigned my position at the facility and passed your file on to one of my colleagues so that I won't have a conflict in any possible relationship we might have in the future." And then, much to his everlasting shock, bemusement and joy, she rose from her chair, bent over him and kissed him on the lips.

Holding his eyes with her face close to his, she said, "I've been in love with you, Pat MacDonnell, pretty much ever since I first met you. I can't tell you why, exactly. There's just this thing about you, this essential goodness that I see in you, and I find it ... *irresistible*. So if you'll have me, I'll be your loving wife."

"I ... I don't ... That is, I don't ..." Pat stammered, though seeing the sting of rejection starting in her eyes, he blurted, "I don't have any experience with … *women!*"

"Oh, bless you. A gentle soul and a virgin, too? But don't you worry, now. I'll teach you all you need to know about sins of the flesh." And when she leaned in to kiss him again, he kissed her back, understanding at last the true meaning of her coyness about him living with her father.

As husband and wife, they officially took over the household, with her father still cheerfully in residence, of course, and they lived happily ever after, too, which for them lasted right up until the moment Andie and the old man were killed in a traffic accident by a drunk driver who crossed the centerline and slammed into them head-on.

Naturally, Pat was devastated by the loss of his wife and "Papa Andy," as he'd taken to calling him, the people who'd helped him find himself and his place in life and given so much of themselves in the process. And, yet, he'd grown strong in the intervening years, and, in his work and his church family that rallied around him and helped him shoulder the burden of his grief as if it were their own, he found solace and healing, and with time, the capacity to forgive his trespasser and even God for his black humor and cruel sense of irony, and to relish his life and the living of it, all while staying in the home he'd shared with his loved ones so he could immerse himself in their spiritual presence and draw sustenance from the memory of their shared happiness.

So, after more than three decades since their deaths and all the mileage that was in them, the only things for which he still bore enmity were Ballyvoo and ferries, and his trip to his childhood home had done nothing to mellow his feelings for either.

For he'd gone to bury the last of his brothers, the eldest of them, who, like a dutiful firstborn had followed in his father's footsteps by quietly drinking himself into oblivion, so quietly, in fact, that it was a month before anyone even thought to look in on him. The other three all died more spectacularly, meaning in violence, that is, one in a bar fight and two in an ambush after joining the local chapter of the Provos (the Provisional Irish Republican Army, that is), which, as it turned out, was riddled with informers. His mother died, too, some years before, though not till after his father, thereby denying the man the satisfaction of ever being free of her. Though given notice each time, Pat went to none of their funerals, fearing that Ballyvoo would infect him with its pestilent hatred and drag him back into its clutches.

Still, as he matured, a pang of guilt grew in him for his boycott, for ministering to so many strangers and yet failing, as he came to see it, to minister to his own family—which was surely in need of healing if anyone ever was—or to even try. Yet, pushing against that was always his sure inner knowledge that any effort on his part would be fruitless anyway, if not downright scorned, so the push ultimately fought the pull of conscience to a standstill and he stayed away. This time, though, it was different, because with his family now gone, he saw an opportunity to bring closure to that part of his life and to atone for his inaction by conducting the funeral service for his brother. Not only that, he would show Ballyvoo that he was proud of the man he'd become and proclaim it by doing something he'd never done before as a minister—he would wear a collar.

But, of course, pride cometh before the fall and the best laid plans, etc., and Ballyvoo welcomed him with low menacing clouds, a steady drizzle and an essential *grayness* that cut to the bone, while his graveside sermon about reconciliation and healing fell on stony ears and brought malevolent stares from the few who turned out, mostly older people that he and his brothers knew in childhood and a couple of ghouls who made a hobby of attending funerals, and he felt their silent hatred cutting him off at the knees like a scythe. Then, afterward, when one of his old tormentors sneered at him, "So Mr. Paisley's gone all Scotch on us, now has he?" he slapped the man so hard that his dentures flew out and shattered on the sidewalk, then shouted, "And you, *boyo*, missed yehr callin' in life when yeh weren't stillborn!"

So Ballyvoo did indeed snare him in its black web, and he boarded the ferry in a dark and destructively introspective mood, feeling that he'd come exactly nowhere and that the life he'd forged for himself was nothing but a sham, a pretty veneer slathered politely over the ugliness that was his birthright. For in that one violent gesture, he'd personified the atavism he so despised and turned his back on everything he believed, everything he'd worked for, everything he'd striven to become, showing himself to be, in his estimation, no better of a human being than those miserable begrudgers he sought to leave behind.

As Pat sat by the window, staring miserably into the dark, turbulent sea and feeling it roiling his gut, he knew that as long as he hated Ballyvoo, he would never be free of it.

THE MAN STOOD BY THE WINDOW of the stern observation deck watching the lights of Belfast disappear behind a curtain of rain and thinking that it wasn't much of a sendoff after he'd spent all those years there pursuing his life's work and chosen destiny. But then, the city was never really home to him, just a long sojourn on a solitary road to somewhere else.

Anyway, all the world would know of his achievement in a few hours, although no one would ever know that it was *him* who did it. Oh, they would search for him, alright, high and low and with every man, woman and resource available to every police, Intelligence and security force in every country, province, city, town and hamlet in the Free World, the Unfree and far beyond. They would call him evil, a mass murderer and a terrorist. They would denounce his act as a *crime against humanity* and liken him to Hitler, Stalin and Mao. No condemnation would be too harsh and no hyperbole too extreme. Justice would be demanded and vows to attain it made. Politicians, preachers and pundits would rail from their respective pulpits, arrests would be made and suspects released for lack of evidence, and many—perhaps *very* many— would make bogus confessions. Through it all, however, they would never find him, never learn his identity, for every trace of the man he'd been for the last ten years would be gone, incinerated in the *phoenix* of his revenge, as dead and buried to the world as the man he'd been in the life he lived before that, and with no clues to follow, no one would even know where to begin the search.

Eventually the hysteria would die down and the passing of many years would relegate it to memory, a faded tapestry as bereft of passion as it would be of color, and though pain would linger for those directly affected, it would die with them and future generations of Irish people, Catholic *and* Protestant, would be able to appreciate the gifts he'd given them—Peace and Unity—and be thankful that some unknown patron had the courage to make the hard choice for them and, thereby, lift the onus of internecine hatred from their shoulders so they could break with the past and embrace their common future. And that would be all the thanks he would ever get or want—a nation of grateful people whom he would never live to see.

All of this, he knew to be true, had known it from the beginning and chose his path with the sure understanding that it was his cross to bear. Yet now that his work was done and he had nothing to occupy his mind while on the ferry, the imagery from the flashback crept obsessively into his thoughts and tormented him with the questions he'd avoided earlier. The more he replayed it in the cinema of his mind, the more certain he became that it was indeed a memory, though he still could not place it into context. Trying to fill in the blank spaces, he thought back to his childhood, when his mother and sister were still alive, to see if he could spark a memory.

Practically speaking, he knew his life to have begun on March 17, 1974, for he remembered little before that beyond a vague sense of happiness and contentment, while the events of that day represented the first step along the road to where he stood. To celebrate St. Patrick's Day, his father drove them into Tucson for Sunday morning mass and the parade that followed, his mother Bridget, his little sister Maeve and himself. It was one of their last family outings together and he recalled it as a very happy day. What stood out, however, was that his father stopped in a small park on the way home, where they got out of their station wagon and stood before the bronze statue of a Spanish Colonial soldier named Hugh O'Conor, whom the

Apache had called *El Capitán Colorado* for his crimson hair, "The Red Captain."

"That's *my* name, too, Daddy!" he'd exclaimed. "I'm Hugh O'Conor, too!"

"Yes, that's right," his father said. "You're named after him and so am I, because he's our ancestor and the oldest sons in our family have always been named after him."

Then his father reverently told the man's story, of how he'd left his home in Ireland at the age of sixteen to enter the service of the King of Spain, that he was made a Knight of Calatrava and rose to the rank of general, became Commandant Inspector of New Spain and Royal Governor of Texas, before founding the city of Tucson.

Little Hugh listened with growing pride as the tale unfolded, while staring into the statue's far-seeing eyes that seemed to focused on him alone and whose pointing finger seemed to say, "I want *you!*" just like those pictures of Uncle Sam he'd seen in the Post Office. Of course, he didn't know what he was wanted for then, just felt the call of duty in his stirring heart.

But the seed of understanding was planted a few weeks later, when Hugh's parents took him and Maeve on an airplane trip all the way to Ireland. Their first stop was at a country manor called Clonalis House, the seat of the O'Conors of Connaught, the ancient royal family to which they belonged. When they introduced themselves and revealed their connection to *El Capitán Colorado*, they were treated like returning royalty and given a private tour of the house by their clan chieftain himself, *The* O'Conor Don, Prince of Connaught. He was a warm and convivial man, a gentleman in every sense of the word, and of course little Hugh was mesmerized to find himself in the company of a real-live prince, especially when he showed them the family heirlooms and a handwritten genealogy of the O'Conors that stretched back through dozens of generations to their noble ancestor, *Conn Céad Cathach*, "Conn of the Hundred Battles," who ruled Ireland as High King in the Second Century A.D and for whom the province of Connaught was named. The lineage of the O'Conors constituted the longest family history in all of Europe, The O'Conor said, with its roots going back to before Jesus walked the Earth. Outside, he showed them the ancient Coronation Stone where, by tradition, newly-elected O'Conor chieftains placed their bare foot into the foot-shaped hollow and ceremonially married themselves to the Land, swearing their allegiance to their clan and their souls to its patrimony.

It was a pivotal experience for Hugh, though it got even better when they moved on to the ruins of Ballintober Castle, the massive fortress where the O'Conor lords held sway for almost four centuries before Oliver Cromwell brought an English army to dispossess them, its high walls and fierce battlements appealing mightily to Hugh's little-boy sense of adventure and romance. It made his heart swell with pride to know that his ancestors were great lords and warriors who lived in such splendor, and he strutted along the crumbling ramparts with his head held high and his eyes attuned to every detail, as if he, himself, were the king surveying his domain.

Afterward, they visited an old cemetery wherein lay a "Famine Grave," which his father explained to be a common burial for people who died during The Great Hunger, a time of national tragedy when countless legions of Irish people either starved to death or fled their homes in terror, scattering across the Earth to far distant lands, heartbroken and never to return. The number who suffered were as many as the stars in the sky and the English imperialists who ruled them barely lifted a finger to help. Rather, they viewed the depopulating of Ireland as a means by which to pacify and subjugate an unruly province. It was a studied inaction that Hugh's father called a "crime against humanity," a *holocaust* as great as that perpetrated by the Nazis upon the Jews, a sort of "final solution to the Irish question." What turned it from an act of Nature into a criminal enterprise of Man, moreover, was that all those who hungered did so in the midst of plenty because they'd been marginalized in their own country and reduced to tenantry on their own land, while their English overlords took the bounty of that land for themselves. As Hugh looked at the dank walls smothered by creeping ivy and grey headstones casting the skeletal shadows of dusk, the image of all those dead people lying pile upon desecrated pile under his feet made him shiver and he could almost feel their ghosts lurking at his elbow. What a horrible place it was and what a horrible calamity to have befallen the Irish, and the magnitude of injustice was evident from his father's passion and indignation.

Their next stop was at the ruins of the old monastery of Clonmacnoise on the River Shannon, where Hugh's father talked about how the Irish were persecuted for their Catholic faith and suffered the indignity the Penal Laws, which basically made it illegal to be a Catholic in Ireland and severely restricted the civil rights of those who persisted.

Then it was on to *Teamhair na Ríogh*, Tara of the Kings, the ancient ceremonial capitol from whence great Conn himself once ruled. As they picnicked on the ground beside the *Lía Fáil*, the Stone of Destiny that was fabled to sing when touched by the true king, Hugh's father told wondrous tales of the ancient Irish and their Heroic Age of legendary kings, queens and champions.

The end of their road took them to Dublin, to yet another burial ground in a place called Glasnevin Churchyard, where were interred the people whom Hugh's father called "our martyrs of freedom," men and women with an honored roll call of names like Emmet, O'Connell, Parnell, Gonne, Booth-Gore, Pearce and many others. As they stood by the solitary grave of Michael Collins, his father remarked that you could "read the history of Ireland's struggle for freedom in the graves of her martyrs," after which he explained how Ireland was divided into two after the War of Independence in 1920, resulting in the "occupied territory" of Ulster remaining part of the United Kingdom and ruled from afar by "strangers" who used the local Protestant majority as their proxies of oppression, another injustice that would be righted only when the "foreigner" was driven out and Ireland united again, one and whole.

The fact that Ireland and the Irish—with whom young Hugh now felt an innate kinship and familial sympathy—had been treated so unjustly, even *cruelly*, by the English became imprinted upon him and it changed his outlook in a way that his parents had not intended. They were kind and gentle people who, as devout Catholic Americans, lived by the teachings of Jesus and the declaration that "all men are created equal," and were raising Hugh according to those values. Moreover, the students of his Catholic school represented a patchwork quilt of races, nationalities and ethnicities, so he'd been exposed to all kinds of people and understood instinctively that everyone was more or less the same. Although cruelty wasn't beyond his experience, it was yet alien and incomprehensible to him, especially as it seemed to have been so purposefully practiced upon the Irish. So as a consequence of his father's stories, he came to think of the English and their allies in the "occupied territory" (the *Orangemen*, as his father called them) in crude tribal terms, as being innately different from himself, "the others" who were to be treated with dread and suspicion.

But it was what happened on their very last day in Ireland that sealed Hugh's fate and set him upon his road in life.

They were in Dublin, walking through a commercial district, Hugh holding his father's hand while his mother carried Maeve in her arms. His mother stopped to look in a shop window while he and his father walked on a few doors ahead. Hearing her call, "Wait for us, silly boys!" he turned just in time to see her and Maeve engulfed in a sudden cataclysm of flame, to lock eyes with her one last time before they vanished from his life forever, before the fury of the blast lifted him from his feet and hurled him onto the sidewalk, where he struck his head and watched in addled fascination as the world went dark around him.

It was four days before he awoke to find himself in a white metal-frame bed with white sheets and blankets, surrounded by white walls and attended by a pale, blond woman dressed all in white. At first, he thought he was dead and in Heaven, floating on a cloud with an angel at his side, until he noticed the multicolored wires running in a tangle from his bandaged head to a bedside monitor and the intravenous tube running to a bag of clear liquid hanging from a metal stand, its steady *drip*, *drip*, *drip* so mesmerizing that it almost lulled him back to sleep.

Seeing that he was conscious, the woman stepped to the doorway, and exclaimed, "Mr. O'Conor! He's awake so!" Then she moved aside as his father—heavily bandaged himself and on crutches—hobbled to his side and clutched him in a fit of sobbing, gasping tears. In that moment of his father's collapse, Hugh saw again the surging fireball devouring his mother and sister (so completely that there was little of them left to bury) and understood instinctively that the terrible image would *never* leave him alone.

He was in the hospital for over a month, as his fractured

skull healed and his faculties slowly returned. But when they weaned him off morphine, he began to have severe headaches when awake and vivid nightmares when asleep, the combination of which left him fatigued, irritable, anxious and unable to concentrate. Even after these symptoms faded and the doctors released him, he was plagued with outbursts of ill temper and an inability to cope with even minor frustration, and his personality changed from happy, friendly and curious to moody, withdrawn and suspicious. Moreover, he found that even moderate stress would bring back the nightmare image and he would be in that place again, watching helplessly as the event unfolded. It made him reluctant to interact with people and he withdrew even further, although his aloneness did little to alleviate the flashbacks.

Somewhat paradoxically, Hugh was relieved when he was allowed to return to school and focus his mind on his studies—on the pedantic progression from page to page, concept to concept and chapter to chapter, as if he were walking along a hedged path and all that mattered was moving forward along it. Where it led, he didn't care, so long as the world left him alone and he took the next step, and the next one, and the next one after that. He was already a grade ahead for his age, but the disciplined abandon with which he threw himself into it drew notice from his sympathetic teachers, who recognized his special needs and allowed him to work independently in the library and progress at his own accelerated pace. He was especially adept at math and science (indeed, almost savant-like), which with their comforting structure and logic fit neatly into his carefully circumscribed world. Yet he trusted no one and allowed no one to get close, and because his temper was vicious and immediate (another reason the teachers separated him from the class), the other children quickly learned to leave him alone. So his remaining years in school were purposefully solitary and he walked through them as indifferent to his fellows as if they didn't exist.

Hugh's time at home, however, was another matter, for his father never recovered emotionally and became distant and reticent himself, and spent increasingly long hours in the safe haven of his foundry, focusing his pain on his work, bending metal to his own shape and design, the one thing in his life over which he exercised unquestioned control, just as his son bent his will upon his schooling. It wasn't that he was either abusive or neglectful—he fed, clothed, housed and schooled Hugh to the best of his ability—yet he was there in body only and *absent* in spirit, his eyes turned inward upon himself and blind to the suffering of his son. So he didn't see how staying late in the foundry—even though it was only a hundred yards from the house—left Hugh vulnerable to the empty hours when he was too exhausted to study any more, but couldn't sleep and had nothing to keep the terrible image at bay.

For his part, Hugh felt both his father's pain and powerless to do anything about it, to bring light into his inner darkness and restore the loving, attentive parent he'd been before. His helplessness made him feel as if his father were stolen from him as completely as his mother and sister, and the anger it caused soon turned to rage, a rage that roiled without object or outlet, for his father was blameless and there was no other target, only the *event*, the *thing* that happened to them because they were in the wrong place at the wrong time, the *tragedy* that he could do nothing about and of which he and his father never spoke, the elephant in the room that united them in the grief that yet kept them apart.

Then one night Hugh awoke in the wee hours and padded toward the kitchen get a drink of water, only to stop short upon finding his father asleep in his recliner before the test pattern-displaying television set, an empty whiskey bottle overturned on the side table. Something about the image caught his eye and, as he waited unconsciously for his mind to make the connection, he remembered noticing that nothing ever seemed to change in his father's bedroom, that even the bed was always made in exactly the same meticulous, precise manner as his mother did it, details he noted in passing without really digesting but which now made him wonder if his father had slept in the room at all in the months since their return, or if he was keeping it purposefully unchanged as a memorial. With that, he understood what it was about the scene that transfixed him, the *loneliness* of it, an aloneness so abject and pitiable that it could drive a man to sleep fully-clothed in a den chair rather than repairing to the soothing comfort of his own room and warm bed because he couldn't bear to be in the place where he'd been intimate and tender with a woman who lived now only in his memory, a memory marred and made grotesque by the heartbreak with which their love story ended.

For a moment, Hugh's anger abated and his heart leapt out to his father, while tears started in his eyes as he stepped forward, meaning to crawl into his lap, throw his arms around him and say, "I love you, Daddy, and I'm still here."

But drawing near, he saw a folder of newspaper clippings lying open on his father's lap, and stopped when his eyes caught the masthead, "THE IRISH TIMES," and the bold headline underneath:

28 KILLED, OVER 100 INJURED IN FOUR CAR-BOMB BLASTS IN DUBLIN, MONAGHAN

In a flash of insight, Hugh knew he would find answers in

those yellowing, dog-eared pages, answers to at least the *what* of it, if not the *who* and the *why*. With that, his rage returned and he longed to scream it out, but instead, just clenched his teeth and forced his emotions down deep inside, gently removed the folder from his father's lap and tiptoed back to his room.

As he poured slowly through the clippings, one by one, a picture of the event and the circumstances surrounding it came into focus in his mind, and although he didn't understand it all, he did at least have the names of the alleged perpetrators—two groups known as the Ulster Volunteer Force (UVF) and the Ulster Defense Association (UDA) that the media called "Protestant paramilitary organizations opposed to the reunification of Ireland" who allegedly acted in concert with elements of the British security forces in Northern Ireland—whom Hugh interpreted to mean "the Orangemen and the English." Gradually, however, his rage cooled to a slow but steady burn, for with that knowledge, it was no longer without object and no longer impotent, because a desire for vengeance sprang up within him, and while he had no concept of how he would attain it, Hugh was determined that it would someday be his.

The next morning, when he laid the folder on the breakfast table beside his father while looking him impassively in the eyes, the man said nothing, just gave him a questioning, tentative look, as if he feared the dialogue that must surely follow and the accompanying agony of scabs ripped from emotional wounds. So he was surprised and relieved when Hugh said, "I don't like being alone at night. So can I work with you in the foundry after school?"

"Alright," he replied, happy to be off the hook and to let the moment pass. "Come in when you finish your homework."

In the foundry, Hugh approached the work in the same disciplined, concerted manner as he did his schooling, while displaying a precocious ability to osmose knowledge and internalize processes and methodologies, to the extent that he could intuit the next step and take it without further direction. His only limitation, initially, was that he just wasn't strong enough for the heavy labor involved. So to compensate, he began lifting weights and running to improve his strength and stamina, and later took up martial arts to improve his reflexes and coordination, these physical pursuits motivated partially, also, by a sense that his desire for retribution would someday require them.

Working side-by-side with his father in this facsimile of companionship brought them each a modicum of comfort, if one unexpressed and mutually unrequited, for they spoke hardly at all beyond necessity, and *never* of their bereavement. Indeed, the only time any sentiment passed between them was the day Hugh received his high school diploma at the age of fifteen, in a private mid-year ceremony in the principal's office, after which his father embraced him self-consciously and said, "I love you, Hugh. And I'm really proud of you."

Tears started in Hugh's eyes and again his heart went out to his father, and in the flow of his long-suppressed emotions, it might even have softened toward the objects of his rage, had not the next moment found the man prostrate on the floor and dying from cardiac arrest, the latest casualty of what posterity had come to call the "Dublin and Monaghan Bombings of May 17, 1974."

With the opening of his father's estate, Hugh discovered that, while the foundry had done little more than support the two of them in modest comfort, his mother was the last heiress of a sizable East-coast fortune (meaning that she'd married his considerably less-affluent father strictly for love, which ratcheted her saintliness up another notch in Hugh's estimation while simultaneously strengthening his resolve), that still had enough money to support him in leisure for the rest of his life, if he so chose. But in his myopic mind, his path was already laid before him and the next step along it would be college, during which the final element in his design for vengeance fell into place in a Middle-Eastern Studies class when he learned of the fragility of the Jewish ethnic majority in Israel and how it could be erased all in one fell swoop. With that, he knew what he would do and the preparations required before his quest could begin in earnest.

The ferry was well out to sea and the going rough, though Hugh barely noticed it, his bent knees unconsciously absorbing the ship's motion as he doggedly scoured his memory for the missing context of his vision. Time was now too short for there to be doubt in his heart or hesitation in his hand, so if anything meaningful were to made of the imagery, he had to do it *soon*!

But then a voice from a few feet away intruded into his ruminations.

"... I *hate* this Goddamn ferry, too, God-*damn* it!"

Turning to the sound, Hugh was shocked to find that the words had come from a *priest*!

AS PAT SAT BY THE WINDOW, staring miserably into the dark turbulent sea and feeling it roiling his gut, he knew that as long as he hated Ballyvoo, he would never be free of it.

"God forgive me but I do so hate that place," he muttered bitterly, then added through clenched teeth, "And, Goddamn it, I *hate* this Goddamn ferry, too, God-*damn* it!" realizing too late that his voice rose along with his spleen.

Glancing furtively about to see if anyone noticed, he saw a man a couple of meters away gaping at him and even though Pat was embarrassed, he had to stifle a grin at his comical expression.

"Oh, sorry, son. Didn't mean to be a namedropper," Pat said, meaning it as a brush-off and intending to turn away.

But the ring of the man's laughter—which was odd and rusty-sounding, as if he hadn't done it in a while—made Pat give him the policeman's once-over, a habit from his old training that he'd never bothered to break. What he saw made him take a second look—a compact athletic build hinting at physical strength (and in a cop's mind, therefore, potential danger), a tattered, faded-out New York Yankee's baseball cap pulled low over his forehead but allowing a fringe of short white hair to needle out underneath, pale, almost-translucent skin and bespectacled eyes the color of blue ice and whose innate coldness were not warmed by the hardness of his jaw, all framed by a beige oxford-cloth shirt open at the neck over a white T-shirt. In short, the man was almost *colorless*, though more in the way of a ghost than an albino, and, as the word formed in Pat's mind, he knew that his laughter was that, too—*colorless*.

"I wouldn't have expected that sort of cynicism from a priest," the man said.

"And yeh didn't get it from one, neither. I'm a Unitarian minister."

"Oh, I see. I could never tell the difference between those collars." Then the man knitted his eyebrows questioningly. "But you look and sound too Irish to be a Proddie."

"A *Proddie*, is it now? And why would an innocent Yank like yehrself use such a hate-colored word?"

"Oh, just something I picked up along the way. No offense." The man started to turn away, meaning to end the conversation himself.

But rather than take the offered out, Pat found himself intrigued, for his instinct, both as a policeman and as a rehab counselor, told him that the man felt as if he'd let some sort of clue slip and Pat wanted to probe deeper.

"What brings yeh to Scotland?" he asked.

"Oh, tourism. Just passing through, you know."

"I live in Glasgow, meself," Pat rejoined quickly, trying to keep him engaged, "though I'm from South Armagh originally. Ballyvoo to be exact."

"Ballyvoo?" the man asked, taking a second look at Pat. "I was there once. Horrible place. Still, if I were born in Ireland, I don't think I could ever leave, no matter where I lived."

"I left *Northern* Ireland, actually. And though it's but an adjective, believe me, it *does* make a difference."

"True. But then, Ulster will be part of the Republic someday. Maybe sooner than you think."

"Not in *my* lifetime, it won't. And, even if it is, there's generations of suspicion and animosity built up that won't evaporate all in a day. Besides, people in the Republic aren't really all that anxious for it to happen, yeh know, in spite o' the noise from the flag-wavers."

"What makes you say that?" the man asked, and Pat noticed that his posture turned more aggressive, as if he didn't like being questioned on the subject. 'Typical Irish-American,' Pat thought, sneering inwardly, 'sure that he knows more about Ireland and what's good for it than them that live there!'

"Because then they'd be stuck with the Proddies, who, as one-sixth o' the population, could make a lot o' trouble if they'd a mind, trouble the good people of the Republic would rather leave to the Brits."

"You mean *you* could make a lot of trouble, don't you?"

"I was born a Catholic and came to Unitarianism by a circuitous route. And, anyway, I live in Scotland now. As I said before."

"So you did. But I'm sure it'll work out better than you think, a united Ireland, that is."

"Yeah, son, and maybe Jasus is comin' back. But I ain't waitin' up nights."

"There it is again," the man said, apparently not finding Pat humorous this time. "Are all Unitarians as cynical as you?"

"No, we're not cynical as a rule, I'd say, though we are pragmatic, and it underlies a good measure of our philosophy."

"Is that why you were in Ireland, then, to convert Catholics to your *pragmatism*?"

"I was there to bury me brother, if yeh're really after knowin'."

"Oh, sorry," the man said, though Pat could tell by his grimace-like grin that he was anything but. "Ah, well, what can you do? But you know what they say—one death is a tragedy, but a million is just a statistic."

"Well, now," Pat said, feeling his Irish coming up. "I'm not sure how to take that. And it's an odd thing to say to a fellah that's grievin'. *Very* odd, indeed."

"Oh, but I didn't say it. Himmler did."

Now Pat was intrigued again, for the remark was both viciously clever and decidedly childish, the sort of deflective riposte he'd heard from both criminals and addicts many times over. He took a deep breath and decided to let the man hang himself with his own words, if he was so inclined.

"No, actually, 'twasn't him neither. T'was a German-Jew author named Kurt Tucholsky that coined it."

"Really? A *Jew* said that? And Himmler quoted him?"

"Sure, the Nazis didn't do much in the way of original thinkin', and they surely didn't discriminate when it came to stealin' that of others. Anyway, it was Stalin that picked it up and ran with it, not Himmler. Not that it makes much of a difference, mind you. They were both full o' the hate."

"And what about Unitarians? What are you full of the hate for?"

"I hate the hatred of Ballyvoo, much as I hate to admit it. And I *especially* hate this Goddamn ferry," Pat finished with a rueful grin.

The man grimace-grinned back at him, with some actual humor in it this time. "You're not like any priest—or *minister*—I've ever met, you know that?"

"Yeah? Well, maybe not. Or, maybe yeh just need to get out more."

"OK, you got me there. But tell me. What made you turn against your own people?"

"Ah, Yank, but yeh've answered yehr question with yehr own. What's so bad about Northern Ireland is that the people are so hopelessly divided by words like 'us' and 'them' that they're blinded to the beauty of the life that's around 'em. Sure, 'tis the perfect example of what I was sayin' about suspicion and animosity and how it won't go away all at once. I left there as soon as ever I could because I saw no hope of it changin', whether Ireland is united someday or not, and I didn't want to spend my life wallowin' in hate, too.

"But look here. I didn't 'turn against me own people,' if by that yer entertainin' some flowery notion o' me betrayin' Irish Nationalism by becomin' a Unitarian. First of all, 'my people,' as yeh put it, aren't just Irish Catholics; they're *all* people, from whatever race, religion or walk o' life they might come. And, second, I came to Unitarianism because o' me desire to help the needy—and, again, not just those from among 'my people,' but *anyone* who's in need—and becomin' a Unitarian minister at the time I did afforded me the best opportunity to serve the most people in the quickest amount of time."

"But why pick a Protestant sect? Couldn't you have done the same as a Catholic priest?"

"Ah, boyo, I don't know. Fate? Circumstance? Opportunity? Because I was a horny wee divil and didn't wanna give up the gooter? Pick one or pick 'em all, it doesn't matter, because it wasn't even about religion. 'T'was about servin' the needs of others. In fact, if the truth be told, I'm not even sure I *believe* in God. And at the tail o' the day, what difference does it make, anyhow?"

"But how can you say that and call yourself a Christian, much less a *minister*?"

"Because I know that the struggle for the human soul isn't fought on a Cosmic scale between the immensities of Good and Evil. It's fought within the human heart between the yin o' self-interest and the yang of doin' right by others. And what that means, as I see it anyway, is that in all of religion—and I do mean *all* of it—there's only one important sentence: 'Do unto others as yeh'd have them do unto you.'"

The man seemed genuinely startled by that, and Pat watched the ice melt in his eyes as they turn inward.

"Just think about it for a minute," he continued softly. "Think about the enormity of what it means. If yeh just lived by that one simple rule, then yeh wouldn't break any o' the Commandments, now would yeh? Yeh wouldn't kill or steal or commit adultery, nor lie nor cheat nor covet nor be envious nor hate. To the contrary, yeh'd feel the pain o' yehr fellah man, and if yeh couldn't help him with it, yeh'd do yehr best endeavor not to make it any worse. And doesn't *that* make yeh a good Christian, whether yeh believe in God and accept Christ as yehr Savior or not? And if yeh're wrong in yehr beliefs but righteous in yehr actions, and if God truly loves yeh, then wouldn't He forgive yeh of yehr pride and willfulness?"

But by the time Pat finished, he knew he'd lost him. Although the man's eyes were wide and staring in a look of comic-horror, it came from something that was playing out inside his own mind. Before Pat could try to reach in and bring him back, the man muttered, "Oh, God. I remember," and lurched quickly away.

Watching him go, Pat thought, "He's up to somethin', that boy, or else he's off his titty-knackers."

Then a more ominous thought occurred to him.

"Or *both*."

HUGH CYCLED THROUGH the brightening gray of dawn along the few kilometers that stretched between Stranraer and Portpatrick, his mind stricken with anxiety and fixated upon the recovered memory that now wouldn't go away.

It was the morning of the bombing in Dublin. After breakfast, they walked to St. Patrick's Cathedral, where they entered a pew, knelt and joined hands to pray together.

"We will say an Our Father," his mother said, and then led them through it.

When they finished and took a seat, she placed Maeve on her lap and turned to Hugh looking very serious. "I want you to understand something, Hugh," she said, "something very important.

"Your Daddy has told you a lot about the history of Ireland and how the Irish people have been mistreated by the English, and everything he told you is true. All of those horrible things really did happen.

"But what I want you to know is that they happened a very long time ago, and that the English people who are alive today had nothing to do with it. So you mustn't be angry with them, and you mustn't *hate* them, because hate is not the answer. Hate never makes anything better. God told us to love one another and to turn the other cheek and to forgive those who trespass against us. And God also gave us the Golden Rule to help us live as good Christians should. Do you remember the Golden Rule? Then say it with me: 'Do unto others as you would have them do unto you.' That's good, Hugh. That's very good.

"So I want you to always follow the Golden Rule and to

think about how other people might feel before you do anything that might hurt them. And if someone does something that hurts you, you must forgive them and love them just like you love your family and your friends.

"Can you do that for me, Hugh? Can you be forgiving and love your fellow man like God wants you to? That's good, Hugh. That's Mommy's good little boy."

There were tears in Hugh's eyes as his mind digested the moment of greatest calamity he'd known since the day of the bombings.

"She doesn't want revenge. She wants me to *forgive* them! How could she possibly want that after what they did to her, to *me*, to all of us? How could she want me to abandon my life's work when I'm on the threshold of success? How could she want that when I've come so far and worked so hard and sacrificed so much? How could she ..."

Then suddenly, there was a horn braying and a car bearing down on him, and he swerved hard to the left ...

MARGARET AGNES GALBRAITH—or "Maggie" as her parents called her even before she was born—didn't consider herself to be a "bad girl." She'd been a good student, after all, a loving daughter, a true friend, a faithful member of the Portpatrick Kirk and had never once been late for work or received so much as a parking fine. In fact, she'd been practically perfect, in her own estimation; indeed, *practically perfect*.

And yet, not quite perfect *enough*, apparently, for here she was with a three-year-old daughter born out of wedlock to a father of whom neither she nor anyone else had had sight or sound since shortly after she told him she was pregnant. The reason for that was that Maggie had a thing for *bad boys*— those leather jacketed, motorcycle-riding, silent, brooding, cigarette-smoking, whiskey-swilling, suffering-for-their-art, James Dean/Mick Jagger misunderstood misfits who could be found hanging around the corners or cruising the streets of a Saturday evening—and the badder they were, the better she liked them, especially if they were pretty and could find their way around the tingly spots of her body.

In the chiseled six feet of sandy-haired, blue-eyed Tony Stuart, Maggie had found the package, right down to the vintage Harley and authentic Iron Cross that dangled from a ball chain around his neck. She first saw him performing in a pub in Stranraer, where she was studying to be a primary school teacher at the local college. He was the frontman for a band that specialized in covering "musical poets" like Dylan, Springsteen, Browne and Cohen, and, when she heard his doleful, tormented version of the latter's *Hallelujah*, she knew that this bad boy was going to be trouble for her. And so he was, for within an hour after the show, she'd presented him with her virginity and, before the night was over, conceived the child that put her on the "Naughty" list of both her male contemporaries in Portpatrick and, more importantly, their gossipy mothers.

Once a doctor confirmed her pregnancy, she took Tony home to meet her father, Graham, with whom she grew up and still lived. "I'm pregnant, Daddy," she said without preamble. "Tony and I are to be married."

"I suppose you mean to have the baby then?" her father asked calmly, having known from the hastily-called meeting and their posture upon entering the house—his hangdog and sheepish and hers anxious but defiant—that good news wasn't in the offing.

"Why, yes, Daddy, of course."

"Alright." Then he turned a probing look onto Tony, whose eyes dropped precipitously to the floor. "So you want to marry my daughter, do you?"

"Yeah, I 'spose," Tony mumbled without conviction. But, feeling both their eyes boring into him, he straightened himself a little and tried again. "I mean, yes ... That is ... Yessir, I do."

"You want *get married*, do you?" Graham confirmed. "You want to get married and sell your motorcycle, settle down and have a family, change dirty nappies, wipe snotty noses, play with whingy brats when you're so tired you can't even see straight? You want to get married, get a steady job, quit drinking, stay home at night, live on a budget, save for a rainy day, go to church every Sunday, have sex once a week, if you're lucky, and once a month after thirty, *and* be responsible for the lives and the feelings of the people who depend on you? You want to get married and do all that, do you? That's what *you*, Tony Stuart, want to do?"

The terror and desperation in Tony's darting eyes, then, were evident even to Maggie. After letting him squirm for a long moment, Graham gave him an out.

"Tell you what, laddie. Why don't you go home and think about it, and we'll talk more tomorrow."

When Maggie rang for Tony the next day, there was no answer, and when she went round to roust him, she found his rented room empty, his bandmates bewildered and no forwarding address. She laid herself down on the bed, then, wrapped herself in the sheets still redolent of their love, and let her heart break. And when she could grieve no more, she sat up, dried her eyes and went home.

"Well, he's gone," she said to her father when he came home that evening. "I hope you're happy with yourself."

"Why, yes, I rather am. Aren't you?"

"Aye, I suppose so. I mean, it would've been a fuckin' disaster, wouldn't it?"

"Watch your language, young lady. But, aye, it would've."

"Still, he was a pretty thing, wasn't he?"

"Aye, he was pretty enough. But pretty is as pretty does, sweetheart."

"Aye. So you've told me, more times than I care to remember. I suppose I should've listened to you."

Then tears started in her eyes.

"But, Daddy. I still want to have the baby."

He pulled her into his embrace and the tears flowed in earnest.

"I'm sorry for disappointing you, Daddy."

"Shhh, hush now. There's no need for that. We all make mistakes in life and there's no way round it. Sometimes they even turn out to be good things. But Maggie, my darlin', my dear. If you want this story to have a happy ending, you're going to have to grow up now. You know that don't you?"

"Aye, Daddy. And I will."

In the months that followed, Maggie finished her schooling and got her degree before her daughter—whom she couldn't help but to name Toni—was born, and, once the child was weaned, she took a job as a Primary 1 teacher in Stranraer. And, while it was hard and she felt at times that her youth had been jerked out of her by the roots, she found life to be good, for the most part. Her father was a prince through it all, the bedrock under her feet, while little Toni—beautiful, loving, lovable, precocious, mesmerizing, *beautiful* little Toni— captured the hearts of everyone who met her, even the overprotective mothers of Portpatrick, who not only moved Maggie back to their "Nice" list, but were not-so-subtly suggesting to their sons that they should bring her round for tea sometime.

Then, too, there'd been the reconciliation with her mother, Jeanne, who lived beyond Stranraer near Cairnryan on the eastern shore of Loch Ryan, but from whom she was mostly estranged since the woman had left her father for another man when Maggie was but two and gone down to New Zealand with him to start a winery/B & B, an idea that sounded wonderfully adventurous to the spontaneous and free-spirited Jeanne but turned out to be anything but in reality. Although the wine part was interesting, the investment was huge, the competition fierce and her dashing Gaelophilic companion, Lochlainn MacLochlainn (she never divorced Graham), proved to be a mercantile baboon. As for the B & B experience, she summed it up by saying, "One does tire of clogged toilets, jezzed-up sheets and serving six a.m. breakfast to surly tourists, you know." She'd come home seven years later dragging her tail and twin sons behind her, chastened and hoping that, having learned from her mistake, Graham might take her back. But he'd adjusted to the life of a single father just fine, thank you very much, and, besides, was not wanting in any way for female company. So, having agreed with him that it might be confusing for Maggie if she suddenly reinserted herself into her life, Jeanne moved in with her mother on the family sheep farm, became a bank clerk and settled in to raise her sons.

When Graham did tell Maggie of her mother's return, she was already old enough to be angry that she'd left in the first place, so despite her father's encouragement, she would have nothing to do with Jeanne through her teen years.

While at university, though, Maggie came into contact with her dashing Gaelophilic half-brothers, Lochlainn Óg and Lulach Dubh, and they became quickly close, although Maggie still held her mother at arm's length. But when Jeanne learned of Maggie's pregnancy, she paid a visit to her and Graham asking to please let her help with the baby.

"I was no mother to you," she said, "and I know there's no way to make it up. But maybe I can make a start it at least."

Maggie looked at her father for guidance. "I think you should let her. She's done very well by your brothers and, frankly, we're going to need the help."

Thinking, 'Oh, what the Hell,' Maggie replied, "Alright, mother. I'm tired of being angry with you. So I forgive you, and you can help. Just don't expect me to suddenly become your loving daughter because that's not going to happen."

They agreed that Jeanne would keep Toni during the day while Maggie was at work, since she lived on the way to Maggie's school and, after her own mother's death, she and her siblings had sold the farm and she now had a degree of financial independence that allowed her to pursue her passion as an artist and work from home. (In a perverse twist of irony, the farm went to a lesbian couple from the Netherlands—"the Dikes of Holland," as the locals came to call them, with many a gibe about sticking in fingers as well as anatomically correct facsimiles of other body parts—who'd fallen in love with Scottish B & B's and wanted to turn the place into one of their own. "Oh, *the humanity*!" Jeanne thought upon hearing their plans, though she'd proceeded with the sale anyway on the theory that "It takes all kinds.") As time passed and Jeanne proved herself a capable and loving grandmother to Toni,

Maggie's reticence eased and they gradually became friendly, to the point that Maggie and Toni would sometimes attend church with her mother and brothers and even stay over for "family supper."

So it was to Jeanne's house and then on to school that Maggie was headed in the early morning, when, coming over a low rise, she saw a bicyclist rise out of the mist before her. Realizing that he was approaching her on the wrong side of the road, she laid on her horn, slammed on her breaks and swerved as far to her left as she could, gasping as he swerved to his own left at the last possible instant and the car slid safely by.

For a moment, all was silent and the only movement was the smoke rising from the angry black skid marks on the faded roadway. In the car, Maggie sat rigidly at attention, with her eyes wide and staring, her heart pounding, her knuckles white on the wheel and her sphincter locked in a death-grip on the car seat. Then Toni's little voice came from beside her, "What's wrong, Mummy?" and she exhaled the breath she'd been holding and forced herself to relax.

"It's alright, darling," she replied shakily, though more to reassure herself than the child. "Everything's OK. There was a man in the road and Mummy didn't want to hit him."

Thinking of the bicyclist then, she glanced in the mirror and saw him picking himself up from the road. Opening the door, she dragged herself from her seat and leaned on the car to steady herself.

"Are you alright?" she called.

"Yes ... Yes I'm fine," he replied. "Are you ... Are you alright?"

"You're a *Yank*?"

"What? Oh. Yes. Yes, I'm an American."

"Did no one tell ever you that we drive on the left side of the road here?"

"What? Oh, yes. Was I ... I mean ... I guess I must've been daydreaming and ... and ... forgot?"

"Aye, I guess you must've." After pausing for a moment to let it come to him, then realizing it wasn't going to, Maggie said, "You need to apologize, you know."

"Oh. Right. I ... I'm really sorry."

"Oh, no. You'll not get off that easily. You need to come *here* and apologize to me *personally*!"

"Oh. Yes. OK then."

He mounted his bicycle and rode toward to her, although he stopped a bit short when he noticed her left rear tyre had gone flat.

"Looks like you've got a flat," he said,

"A what?"

"A flat. I mean a *puncture*. You've got a puncture."

"Ohhhh," she groaned, coming around to take a look for herself. "Now you *really* need to apologize."

"Yes, I suppose I do, don't I?" Drawing himself up formally as best he could while astride the bike, he began, "I sinc ..."

"No, I said personally."

"What?"

"I said *personally*. That means you have to say my name."

"Oh. Uh ... OK. What's your name?"

"Maggie Galbraith," she said, extending her hand for him to shake. "What's yours."

For a moment, he seemed dumbfounded, and stared at her as if she'd asked him the precise length of his male appendage.

"Forgot your own name, have you?" she teased. "Am I as beautiful as all that?"

"No. I mean *yes*! I mean ... I ..."

At that moment, Toni called, "Mummy, what are you doing?"

Turning to see her climbing from the car, Maggie scooped her into her arms and bussed her cheek.

"Oh, Toni dear, we've had a puncture. But don't worry. This

nice man is going to fix it for us, and then we'll be on our way, spit-spot."

"Spit-spot!" Toni parroted.

"Spit-spot," Maggie agreed.

Glancing at the man, she saw the spellbound look on his face that people often sported upon seeing Toni for the first time, with her bundle of blonde curls, blue eyes and heartbreaking sweetness. She gave him a moment to drink it in, before saying, "You'd better get busy, Mr. No-name. I can't be late to school."

"What? Oh, I can't … I don't … That is, I … I have to …"

"Always this tongue-tied, are you?"

He opened his mouth to answer, but closed it again, took a deep breath and let it out slowly. "Not usually. Do you always have this affect on people."

"Not on people, no," she replied, fluttering her eyelashes and flashing him a teasing smile. "Only on men."

He smiled, too, then, though it seemed to her that he did so with effort and in spite of himself.

"Um, the tyre?" she reminded him. "You do know how to change a tyre don't you?"

"Oh, yes. But … but … I can't …"

"Come on now. I mean, how would you feel if I'd run *you* off the road and given you a puncture?"

At that, his eyes went far away, as if he were seeing things from another place and time. "Yeah, sure," he said finally. "But I don't have much time."

"Well, then, get on with you. The spare and jack are in the boot."

He set to it in earnest then, and Maggie could only marvel at his skill and proficiency, the way he calmly assayed the problem and directed his economical movements in precise choreography with his plan of attack, his efficient hands and mind dancing in such expert harmony that he had the job done and the boot closed in less than ten minutes. And though his performance was almost-robotic in quality, there was yet an innate artistry to it that left Maggie feeling rather breathless, like … well, like she had when watching Tony sing.

"That was *amazing!*" she exclaimed. "Where did you learn to work like that?"

But he just shrugged. "I really have to go now."

"Oh. OK," she said, finding herself curiously disappointed. "But aren't you forgetting something?"

"What?"

"My apology?"

"Oh. Yeah. Maggie Galbraith, I sinc …"

"You have to take off your hat." The words came from Toni and he gaped at her uncomprehendingly.

"What, dear?" Maggie asked.

"He has to take off his hat, Mummy! Grampa says a gentleman should always take off his hat to a lady."

"Oh, sorry," Maggie said. "It's a game they play."

He hesitated, looking wretchedly and incongruously indecisive, before slowly bearing his head.

"Oh, my!" Maggie exclaimed. "Look at all that hair. I thought you'd be bald under your wee caubeen. But you have to grow it longer. It makes you look so dowdy that way, what with it being white and all."

For a moment he looked so miserable that Maggie thought to apologize herself. But before she could, he intoned solemnly, "Miss Maggie Galbraith, I sincerely apologize for my negligence and for any inconvenience it might've caused you."

"Apology accepted, Mr. No-name. And thank you for changing the tyre and being such a gentleman."

"You're welcome," he said, then just stood there staring at her, seemingly at a loss for what to do.

"Well, go on with you," Maggie prodded gently. "You were in such a hurry …"

"Oh. Right. Goodbye, then. And goodbye, Toni."

"Goodbye, Mr. No-name. Come back when the wind changes."

He smiled again then, though unselfconsciously this time, naturally, as if he really felt it in his heart, and, when Maggie saw how it warmed his face, she thought, "My, he's really quite pretty in an older-fellah sort of way."

"*Mary Poppins*, right?" he asked Toni. "My mother took me to see it when I was a little boy—just about your age."

His eyes turned inward and far away then, as he said softly, "I still remember the dress she wore and the way she held me in her lap, the smell of her perfume and ... and ..."

Coming back to the present, with his eyes still on Toni, he said, "She's the most *impossibly* beautiful thing I've ever seen ..." before shifting them to Maggie, "... other than you."

Feeling herself go warm and squishy in a way she hadn't since Tony, Maggie said, "*My*, but you do know what to say to a girl, now don't you?"

He blushed himself then and hurriedly mounted his bicycle. But before departing, he looked at Maggie again. "It's Hugh."

"What? It's *me*? What do you mean by that?"

"No, no. Not *you*. *Hhhugh*. My name is Hugh."

"Oh, *Hhhugh*. Hugh what?"

But he didn't answer, just turned and rode away.

Watching him go, Maggie hugged Toni to her tightly, almost defensively, in the same way as she'd hugged the pillow in Tony's bed after his desertion, as if to defend herself from loss.

"Oh, well," she sighed. "I guess he'll always be 'Mr. No-name' to us."

"I like him," Toni said. "He's a gentleman."

"Aye, there's nothing *bad* about that boy, now is there?" Maggie said, watching as he rode over the rise and disappeared from view.

"Do you like him, Mummy?"

"Aye, Toni dear, I suppose so. But you know what Mary Poppins says—"Practically perfect people never permit sentiment to muddle their thinking."

STANDING IN THE RED PUBLIC PHONE BOX near the harbor in Portpatrick, Hugh knew that he'd come to the end of his road. All he had to do was pick up the phone, punch in his home number, wait for the answering machine and enter the detonation code. *Boom* and it would be done, and he would have his revenge and the oppressed Catholics of Northern Ireland would be free!

Free!

Free? It occurred to him that, until that very moment, he'd never known that freedom meant he was free to choose his own road—whether to follow the one he was on or to take a new one. The visions of his mother impelling him to vengeance were just tricks of his injured brain, after all, ephemera that he'd seen only in hallucinations and never in real life. What was *real* was his memory of his mother as she really was—kind, gentle, loving and forgiving. She was a Christian in name and in deed, a woman who fought the righteous battle between self-interest and doing right by others in her own heart, and Hugh knew that she would be horrified and *deeply* saddened to know of how he'd spent his life.

Her ending made him think of all the mothers and children he'd seen in Belfast and of them evaporating in *his* holocaust, some so suddenly that they wouldn't even register the thought, others slowly and in torment from horrific injuries, while still others were eaten alive by cancers years or even decades later, or, though physically uninjured, would slaughter themselves to escape the abiding emotional and psychological torture. And for what, in the end? So he could exact his personal vengeance while killing enough Protestants to end their majority and leave the Brits no excuse for holding Ulster? Did he really need revenge, and was there no other way to reconciliation in

Northern Ireland?

Thinking of Maggie and Toni, Hugh asked himself aloud, "If they were in Belfast right now, would I detonate the bomb?"

As the reply crossed his lips, he shook his head and smiled, smiled a smile that stretched his cheeks and lit up his eyes as well as his heart of darkness. Then it turned to laughter and he laughed as he hadn't since he was a child, laughed from his soul with pure, hundred-proof joy. He was at peace in that moment, and the only image his calm mind held was Maggie holding Toni in her arms and the two of them beautiful and smiling.

Hugh's laughter faded but his smile remained, though it took a turn toward sadness. It was time to *act!* There could be neither doubt in his heart nor hesitation in his hand. He'd come too far to let his will fail him now.

Hugh picked up the phone and began to punch in the number.

PAT MacDONNELL sat at his breakfast table going over his conversation with the man on the ferry and examining the clues and salient points to see if they added up to the same conclusion he'd come to the time before, and the time before that. He'd even written it down more or less verbatim, a skill honed by his police training and the years spent as a counselor taking notes from interviews and then considering the words in light of the circumstances and the nuances of the respondent's affect and behavior. It was amazing how much people would reveal if you could get them to talk, even when they didn't mean to, and amazing how much detail one's subconscious would reveal upon reexamination. Still it came down to a luck shot with this fellow, the random mention of Ballyvoo that got him to stand still and allow Pat to suck him in so he could follow up on the first clue—the man's apparent feeling that he'd let something potentially incriminating slip in saying "You look and sound too Irish to be a *Proddie,*" and the second—his reticence to converse any further lest he do it again.

From that, Pat gleaned a wealth of information, including the man's obvious allegiance to the Catholic/Nationalist cause in Northern Ireland, as well as that he'd said it to someone whom he thought *was* a Proddie, meaning that he didn't care that Pat might be offended by it. Given his open, non-defensive posture, Pat also inferred that he had no fear of Pat taking physical or any other sort of exception to the insult. And what kind of a man has no fear of being smacked in his clinkers? One who is either mentally deranged or has absolute confidence in his ability to defend himself. But mental defect is arbitrary and, therefore, an investigatory dead end, whereas confidence in one's fighting ability comes from training and experience, things that could be acquired through peaceful means like athletics or kung fu lessons, but also from service in the armed forces or membership in a criminal gang or paramilitary group, all of which fit with his compact athletic build that spoke of physical strength.

So from this and the man's generally aggressive tone, Pat felt comfortable in hypothesizing that he was an Irish-American Catholic who had some sort of military or paramilitary training, that he was using it in some sort of clandestine way to further the interests of the Nationalist cause in Northern Ireland and that he might, *might*, be involved in a current operation. But while that might be solid deductive police work, did it add up to what he'd read in the morning newspaper?

Pat retrieved the front page from atop his untouched breakfast and reread the parts he'd highlighted.

NUKE IN BELFAST
IRA SUSPECTED
Rioting in the Shankill. Peace Walls Breached.
The Falls Road in Flames. Random Killings of Catholics.
Manhunt for Mastermind.

In connection with what authorities are calling a demonic and depraved scheme to unite Ireland by killing Protestants en masse, the Prime Minister has declared a State of Emergency in Northern Ireland.

Hundreds of suspected Irish Republican Army operatives and sympathizers have been detained for questioning in maximum security lockups throughout the province.

A massive manhunt involving the police, armed forces

and security apparatus of the United Kingdom and the Irish Republic is underway to find the suspected mastermind, alleged IRA operative William Johnston, a resident of East Belfast. Johnston is also known by the pseudonym of "Feardorcha" (which means "the dark man" in Irish) that he used in his work as a sculptor, and may have other aliases, as well. Though his present whereabouts are unknown, it is possible that he has left Ireland.

Johnston is described as a white male forty to forty-five years old, about six feet tall and twelve to thirteen stone, with long black hair, hazel eyes, pale skin and a heavy black beard. No photographs have been found of him, but the Royal Ulster Constabulary have provided a composite sketch.

Johnston appears to have no friends or traceable family and those who live in his neighborhood describe him as an "odd bird" who kept entirely to himself. According to his art dealer, Johnston's clients are wealthy Middle-Eastern Muslims from Arab nations. Authorities from both the U.K. and the countries in question are interviewing these people for possible connections to the plot.

Johnston is a skilled foundryman and metal worker and is thought to have some detailed knowledge of chemistry and physics. He is considered highly intelligent as well as armed and extremely dangerous.

Detective-Superintendent Alistair McCook of the Royal Ulster Constabulary is in command of the investigation. When asked what charges might be brought against Johnston, McCook said, "The list of crimes committed is too long to recite. However, because of the deaths in the rioting, we will also consider felony-murder."

As they had when he first read the article, the words leapt from Pat's memory and flashed in his consciousness like tawdry neon hawking a peep show:

"One death is a tragedy, whereas a million is a statistic."

"Ulster will be part of the Republic someday. Maybe sooner than you think."

"A million deaths and Ireland soon-to-be-united," Pat thought aloud. "I thought he might be up to somethin' but, *Jazis*, who'd have thought this? But will anyone believe me?"

THE TRANSCRIPT OF THE CALL received at the RUC
Emergency Response Center read as follows:

Officer: Please state your name and the location and
nature of your emergency.

Caller: Are we bein' recorded?

Officer: Yes, we're being recorded. Please state your
name and the ...

Caller: I want to report a bomb at 12 McDowell Street in
East Belfast. It's sittin' on the work bench in the studio and
looks like a sculpture of a lady holdin' her daughter. Also—
and listen to this very carefully—the bomb is *nuclear*!

Officer: Did you say the bomb is *nuclear*?

Caller: It is nuclear and I am not, repeat, *not* jokin'!

Officer: What is your name and ...

Caller: Don't interrupt again. I'm goin' to give yeh very
specific instructions for how to disarm it. Once that's done,
the warhead will be safe to move to a secure location. But
yeh're goin' to have to hurry because at noon a failsafe
timer will detonate it automatically.

(The instructions followed then, with the caller speaking
clearly and concisely.)

Caller: That's it so. I hope yeh got it.

Officer: Yes, we have it. But please stay on the ...

Caller terminates connection.

Officer: Did you get a trace on that?

Technician: No.

LIKE THE REVEREND Ian Patrick MacDonnell, Detective-Superintendent Alistair McCook of the Royal Ulster Constabulary had a problem with his name, though not due to its obvious similarity to the one of that Brit on American telly, but because of the travesty the Sesame Street people had made of it with their "Monsterpiece Theatre" parody and it's "Me Alistair Cookie" line. They hadn't aimed it at him personally and he knew it, of course, but all it took was for one young officer to watch the show with his wee ones and McCook's nickname of "Cookie Monster" was born. Though none of his junior officers dared say it within his hearing, it stuck to him like gum on his gumshoe shoes, and he was known as such throughout the force. Had he been a bit less ambitious and, therefore, less *paranoid*, he would've seen that the reputation he'd garnered from being the youngest man in the history of the RUC to make Detective Superintendent—and that because of his ability to chew through cases like ... well, like Cookie Monster through macaroons—led the rank and file to speak of him almost hagiographically, no matter what they called him.

Yet, it wasn't his subordinates that concerned him, but the senior officers, for he knew he had a chance to rise high himself—perhaps even to the top—and that they would be the ones to decide his fate, and how could *anyone* take him seriously when *everyone* called him "Cookie Monster?!" Indeed, he quivered with anticipated humiliation whenever he imagined himself receiving his knighthood from the Queen and her lumbering oaf of a consort (he of the "born with a silver foot in his mouth" repute) saying something inane but disastrous like "I dub thee Sir Cookie Monster, Lord of Sesame Street!"

But he also knew that a speed ramp had been laid on his

path to knighthood with this latest case, although it came as no surprise, considering its nature and the fact that he was simply the best the RUC had to offer.

"The Prime Minister and I have the utmost confidence in you, Cookie," the Chief Constable had said in his best glad-handing-politician, Queen's-English idiolect. "We know you always get your man!"

"Jesus," McCook thought, "could he *be* any more of a knab?" Aloud, he said, "Yes sir, I'll go out and win one for the Gipper!" meaning to be surreptitiously sarcastic, only to be met with a bewildered look on the Chief's face.

"Win one for the *what*?" he asked, and McCook's spirits sank in anticipation of the tiresome explanation he knew must follow. Luckily, however, the Chief's self-important little sparrow-fart of an assistant jumped in with a rapid and encyclopedic recitation of the connection to Ronald Reagan (whom, as a Thatcher-phile, the Chief greatly admired), at the end of which the Chief smiled in delighted and faux-humble enlightenment.

"Ah, yes. I see," he said. "Jolly good, that. Yes, do go out and win one for the Gipper!"

As he left the office, McCook made a mental note to never again waste his time trying to patronize a ninny.

Still, he had to admit that the Chief was right in his assessment—he had a hound-like ability to hunt his quarry to earth and only a very lucky few had slipped through his fingers over the years, and none of those permanently. But he also knew that if he failed to solve this one, it would ruin him. Well, "ruin" was perhaps a strong word, but he would certainly go no higher in the ranks and, over time, would gradually be stripped of responsibility and authority until he had nothing to do all day but sit at his desk and pick his nose, retiring, in the end, from the sheer weight of ennui. Worse than that, even, he'd be pilloried in the press as the man who failed to crack *The*

Fiendish Plot of Dr. Fu MacChu, as the locals had dubbed it in their black, gallows humor. All of which only went to show that, just as no good deed goes unpunished, there is sometimes a price to pay for the privilege of being the best.

On the other hand, if he *did* get him, then his path to Chief Constable and Knighthood (and perhaps even that new Jaguar he'd always coveted) would be significantly shortened. But the operative word there was *if*, and as he sat at his desk rubbing his sleep-deprived eyes, McCook began to think that this one might be beyond his reach.

Despite the capacious quantity of information collected, the actual facts to go on were few: The bomb threat was called in by a male who spoke with an Irish accent, most likely of Ulster origin; the bomb was found in the heart of East Belfast right where the caller said it would be; and the bomb was indeed nuclear and had an explosive capacity sufficient to kill most everyone in East Belfast.

About William Johnston himself, next to nothing was known for certain and the little that had come to light only raised more questions. To begin with, since no records of any sort predated that time, he seemed to have sprung from thin air just over ten years ago when he bought the defunct foundry at a bankruptcy auction and turned it into an artist's studio. He paid by a cashier's cheque drawn on an Isle of Man account, which was opened shortly before the purchase in the name of Johnston Investments, Ltd. and closed immediately thereafter, with no surviving records showing to whom the balance of the funds were dispersed and none relating to Johnston Investments, Ltd. to be found anywhere.

He never applied for a driving permit or passport, nor were identifying documents of any sort found at the scene. He had no traceable family or relations, and his only known associate, his art dealer, had never met him in person. As yet, no photographs of him had been found and the sketch compiled from descriptions showed him with long dark hair, a heavy beard and one of those Australian oilskin hats pulled low over his bespectacled eyes, meaning that if he'd changed his appearance even in the slightest, he would be extremely difficult to identify.

Assuming that the caller, the bomb-maker and William Johnston/Feardorcha were all one and the same (which was by no means certain and seemed improbable given the complexities involved), he was an expert metal worker and foundryman possessed of a working understanding of metallurgy, machinery, chemistry and physics, all while having a deep artistic sensibility and exquisite dexterity. His facility with disguises, developing a backstory and breaking connections with previous identities, as well as his disciplined ability to stay in character for an extended period of time, suggested some sort of Intelligence training. He had a ruthless streak that enabled him to plan murder on a mass scale, though it was counterbalanced by a conscience that ultimately wouldn't let him go through with it.

Both the UDA and UVF had checked him out over the years, and, finding nothing amiss, shook him down for protection money, which he paid promptly and with never a complaint. Johnston had no close neighbors because his foundry was located in a dilapidated commercial area. People often saw him walking in the rain but thought he was just some sort of leftover hippie and gone a bit daft from the drugs. He was soft-spoken in shops and unfailingly polite but never chatted with anyone. No one had seen him leave his place before the call, there'd been no sightings in taxies, on ferries, at airports or bus or train terminals, nor any at the border with Éire. The *Garda Síochána* and G2 had turned up nothing, nor had MI5, MI6, Scotland Yard, nor the CIA or FBI.

Two bank accounts had been found for him thus far, a personal one in Belfast under the name of "William Johnston," and a business one in Dublin under the name of "Feardorcha Art, Ltd.", on which William Johnston was the sole signatory. The latter was funded exclusively by deposits from Johnston's Dublin art dealer, Éamon Perrot, from which, in turn, deposits were made to the Belfast account.

It was Perrot who confirmed Johnston and Feardorcha the sculptor to be one and the same. He also stated that Feardorcha's collectors were all wealthy Arabs and that the pieces sold for £100,000 or more, depending upon the size. Only one or two were produced annually—all strictly on commission—and Perrot had never had one in inventory, though he had a sizable waiting list with 50% down-payments in hand and was frantic that he'd now have to refund the money, three-fourths of which went to Johnston up-front and his portion of which he'd mostly spent. All the pieces were interpretations of Bríd, the Irish fire goddess, enveloped in flame and were titled "Bríd I," "Bríd II," et cetera. All incorporated an exquisitely detailed and rendered naked woman with gold, silver, copper and platinum sheathing over bronze, which he apparently cast himself.

Aside from not meeting in person, Perrot had never been given a photograph, résumé, artist's statement or any other kind of background data. Johnston just called out of the blue one day with the name and contact information of the first buyer, a prominent Saudi prince (who'd since been assassinated), and asked Perrot to broker the deal and arrange for shipping and collections. He said the prince was well-connected in the Middle East and that word of mouth would bring more sales. When Perrot asked why he didn't do it himself and save the commission, Johnston said he just wanted to make art and not be bothered with the business end of it. And, with £25,000 per piece in play, Perrot just closed his mouth and did what he was told. After that, he had to work a bit harder for it, since Johnston wanted him to handle his other affairs related to the business of producing his art, though it was still the easiest—and most—money Perrot had ever made as an art dealer.

Handwriting analysis from Johnston's cheques showed him to be left-handed, highly intelligent, emotionally stable with a balanced self-image, honest, physically active and artistic, although given the size and nature of the sampling, none of the inferences were considered conclusive. In fact, it seemed to the analyst as if he'd purposefully "forged" his own handwriting in a way that would show nothing aberrant about his personality or identity and maintain his anonymity, which was another indicator of Intelligence training.

But perhaps the strangest thing uncovered thus far had to do with finger prints, for while forensics turned up dozens of sets in the old foundry, none could be specifically identified as William Johnston's because cross-checks on documents at his banks and art dealer—the only other known sources—had found only the prints of bank employees and Perrot, respectively. That meant one of two things—that Johnston had gone to extreme measures *for over a decade* to leave no fingerprints in his wake or that he'd had them removed. McCook knew that the American gangster, John Dillinger, removed his with acid so they couldn't tie him to crime scenes. But even if their man were crazy and/or committed enough to endure that kind of pain, wouldn't it inhibit the practice of his artistry?

Or what if …

At that moment, McCook's intercom buzzed and he swore as the thought forming in his weary mind suddenly evaporated.

"*What*, Janice," he snarled.

"Sir, it's Finn Casey calling from Dublin."

At that, McCook's spirits rose, for Casey was a Superintendent with the *Garda Síochána*, his equivalent in rank and unofficial liaison to the Republic. They were on friendly terms personally and met at least once a year to play a round of golf and keep the communication flowing.

"Good. Put him through."

"Hello, Finn. How are you?"

"Grand so, Cookie. And yehrself?"

"Up to my arse in alligators, as our American friends would say. I suppose you're calling about "Dr. Fu MacChu," as they've dubbed him up here?"

"Is that what they're callin' him, now?" Casey chuckled. "Brilliant! But, yeah, I've got a fellah that wants to talk to yeh about him. He's an old friend from the *Gardaí*. Walked the beat with me in North Dublin back in the day. Says he might've seen yehr man, MacChu, on the Belfast-Stranraer ferry two nights ago. Says he can work up a sketch for yeh, too. Honestly, from what he tells me, it sounds like a long shot, but if I was walkin' in yeh're brogues, I'd give him an ear."

"Sure, Finn, if you say so. Put him on then."

"Oh, I don't have him *here*, mind you. Fact is, he's in yehr outer office right now. Yehr secretary tried to make him go through channels and he called me to grease the skids."

"A Garda is in my outer office and Janice wouldn't let him in? I'll have to smack the silly bitch for that."

"Oh, he's not one ours anymore. Fact is, he was tossed on his ear for gettin' pissed on the job and floggin' the Gallopin' Hogan out of a suspect, a drug dealer that raped a young one. Got himself cleaned up after, though, and he's been a Unitarian minister in Glasgow the thirty years since. Not sure that last bit says much for his character so."

McCook chuckled in turn. "No, maybe not. What's his name?"

"Well, I knew him as "Paddy" MacDonnell but he says he goes by "Pat" now."

"You *knew* him, you say? How long has it been since you've seen him?"

"Last time was just before he moved to Glasgow."

"Thirty years ago?   And why did he call you, specifically, after all that time?"

"Yyyeahhh, let's just say I owed him one and let it go at that."

"Fair enough. If anything comes of it, I'll owe you."

"Right-O. Regards to the missus."

"And yours."

McCook replaced the receiver and went to open the door of his office, from where he saw a tall, broad-shouldered, distinguished-looking, sixty-something man standing just beyond his secretary's purview and gazing back at him intently. "Reverend MacDonnell?" he asked.

"Aye, himself," the man replied.

"Please come in."

Closing the door behind them, McCook shook hands with Pat and exchanged formalities, then showed him to a chair and returned to his seat behind his desk.

"So, Reverend, Finn says you might have something for me."

"It's just plain "Pat," if yeh don't mind. And, sure, I might, and I emphasize *might* because I've been off the job for more than thirty years now."

"So Finn told me."

"And did he also tell yeh how I left it?"

"He did. But no worries there. But for the drinking, I'd have given you a medal."

"Oh, no, laddie. 'Twas no hero I was, and what I did was surely nothin' to be proud of."

McCook just shrugged, having heard exactly what he wanted to hear. "But you're a Unitarian, are you? That must've been a rare thing in Dublin."

Pat grinned. "No, yeh've got it wrong there, Detective. I'm a Taig from Ballyvoo in South Armagh. I followed a rocky road to Dublin and made me own path from there."

"Ballyvoo? You have my condolences. I wouldn't wish that

76

hoaching sty on my worst enemy, Taig *or* Proddie."

Pat's grin broadened and McCook couldn't help himself but to return it.

"I think we understand each other, Superintendent."

"Just plain Alistair will do, at least in here anyway. But, alright. Give me what you've got."

"OK. First of all, by his speech and manner, he's not Irish but American, although certainly of the 'hyphenated' sort."

"An Irish-American? Are you sure?"

"Yeah, as much as I can be. And he was posin' as a tourist. Even had on an oul' New York Yankees hat to complete the getup."

McCook nodded appraisingly, appreciating the caveat as much as the information. A good detective could never be one-hundred percent sure about anything in an investigation like this and when dealing with such a sophisticated suspect, and Pat's reservation showed that he was thinking like a cop, which took him up a notch in McCook's estimation.

"Alright," he said, grabbing his pad and pen. "What's he look like?"

"White, Northwest European, forty give or take, six feet, thirteen stone, compact, athletic, ice blue eyes, heavy-rimmed glasses, pale skin, buzzed white hair—at least around the fringes, anyway, 'cause he never doffed his caubeen."

"You've read the newspaper, I assume?" McCook asked.

"Aye, and I know some of that fits and some of it doesn't. That's all part of why I came to see yeh in person."

"Anything else?"

"He's military, I would say, possibly special forces of some sort, or a sniper or even an assassin maybe. That's because his eyes were cold and locked in on yeh like he'd already decided how he'd snuff yeh, if it came to it. At least they were so in the beginnin' anyway, though they changed by the time we finished talkin', profoundly almost, as if he suddenly turned warm-blooded on me."

"What did you do, evangelize him?"

"In a manner of speakin', yeh might say. But I think a better way to put it is that I gave him somethin' to think about that might've changed his mind on a thing or two. After all, he didn't go through with it, yeh know, not that I'm after takin' credit for it, now, mind yeh."

"Good point. What makes you think he's MacChu?"

"Who?"

"Oh, sorry. I haven't slept in a while. That's what they're calling this around Belfast—*The Fiendish Plot of Dr. Fu MacChu*."

"Oh, I see. Brilliant! OK. Well, that's the other reason I came in person and had Finn present me callin' card, because I'm goin' to be the first to admit that, by itself, it's somethin' of a stretch. But here we go."

Without referring to his notes, Pat ran McCook through the conversation, telling him that he'd suspected the man was either up to something or a bit mad. In support of that he told him about all his years as an addiction counselor and how, in conjunction with his police training, it had made him sensitive to the subtlest nuances in a person's demeanor, especially when they weren't being forthcoming, which addicts rarely were. He also told him that the man seemed unused to extended conversations, like someone who'd "kept entirely to himself" for a long time. Then he connected the dots between his aggressive tone and devil-may-care attitude, a million deaths, a soon-to-be-united-Ireland and the fact that a nuclear device strategically placed in the heart of East Belfast would kill enough Protestants to give Ulster a Catholic majority and end Partition.

At the end, Pat told of the change in the man's demeanor after they'd talked about the Golden Rule and how the battle for the human soul is fought in the human heart, saying, "I did that on purpose, thinkin', as I was, that he was up to somethin'. But I could never have guessed that he might be up to this, mind you."

McCook laid down his pen, pursed his lips and looked contemplatively at Pat. "One question. Why did you take the ferry to Stranraer rather than Troon? You wouldn't have had to drive as far."

Pat shrugged. "Aye, well, yeh know how that fellah, Sartre, said that 'Hell is other people?' Well, he never crossed the Irish Sea on a ferryboat!"

"Get a bit queasy, do you?"

"Yeh might say so."

"I see. Well, Pat, I can't fault your logic, or your detective work, though, speaking frankly, you're right—it *is* a stretch. But then, I'm a pretty good detective myself, and I have a hunch you just might be onto something. So lets get you with the sketch artist and see what turns up."

"Sure, but there's one more thing first. He's not IRA, yeh know."

"Oh, and why would you say that?"

"Ah, Superintendent, here we are gettin' chummy with each other and then yeh want to go and patronize me. Look. I know he's not and I know *you* know it, too, because I know as well as you do that the IRA are rotten with informers from top to bottom and back again, and the reason I know that is because two o' me own brothers—foolish lads that they were—were done in by rats in the Ballyvoo Brigade, and, if yeh can turn a lad in a tribal, fratricidal place like that, God only knows what yeh've done with the civilized ones up here in Belfast. So let's drop the pretenses, shall we? You know he's a lone wolf because yehr fellahs on the inside have told yeh so, and, even if they hadn't, yeh know as well as I do that the Provos could never keep a secret of an operation like this, poor clumsy fellahs that they are.

"So, that bein' the case, yeh had no reason to drag 'em all in like yeh did and leave the Catholics defenseless against the mob. And meanin' no offense, now, to you and yehrs here at RUC, but that *is* the practical reality of things, that the Catholics are swingin' in the breeze without the Provos standin' up for 'em. Sure, I know yeh had to scoop up some of 'em just for show and the sake o' peace with yehr own community, but if yeh were goin' to drag 'em *all* in, yeh should've taken the UDA and the UVF off the streets, too, just to level the playin' field."

"Well, if it's any consolation to you, Reverend, it wasn't my idea to arrest them. In fact, the Prime Minister and even the Chief Constable wanted to keep the operation on the quiet, just so this sort of thing—'civil war,' as they put it—wouldn't happen. But, being the knowledgeable fellow you are, you know we're riddled with UDA and UVF men, ourselves, so it was all out in the wind with fingers pointed before anyone could do anything about it. And as for dragging them in ..." McCook threw up his hands in a gesture of futility.

"Sure, and how did I *know* yeh were goin' to say that?" Pat said, without sparing the sarcasm. "Innocent people are dyin' out there, Detective, and if yeh don't or *won't* enforce the law equally to protect 'em, then why did yeh become a peeler in the first place?"

McCook's first inclination was indignation, though his professional discretion held him in check just long enough for him to see the justice in Pat's words. He took a deep breath and let it out slowly.

"Reverend, between us and the four walls, I think the IRA and their Protestant counterparts are all just a bunch of thugs and petty criminals and represent the true impediments to peace and reconciliation in this province. If it were up to me, I'd put the lot of them in a boat and sink it. But I can't. I'm bound by the legal and political realities of the situation, and I have to work for justice within them as best I can."

"Not the way, I see it, yeh don't," Pat said, grinning slyly.

"What do you mean?"

"Yeh're in charge of findin' the suspect, are yeh not?"

"Yes, but ..."

"And with the State of Emergency in place, that means yeh're the most powerful man in Northern Ireland and can do pretty much anything yeh want to in the name of that responsibility, doesn't it?"

"Well ... I suppose so. I mean ... Now that you mention it ..."

"So get up a squad o' constables that're loyal to yeh, have 'em arrest the big fellahs in the UDA and UVF and hold 'em in a secure location that only you know about. Then put out the story that yeh've got credible evidence to suggest that the whole thing might've been a Loyalist setup designed to discredit the Nationalists—which was why the bomb wasn't exploded, etc.—and, bein' the good detective yeh are, yeh have to investigate all possible leads. Meanwhile, sweat yehr prisoners into makin' a statement on telly to call off the mob. Yeh must have somethin' on at least one of 'em yeh can use for leverage."

"And if I don't?"

"Then issue a statement in their names anyway. As long as yeh have 'em incommunicado, what difference does it make?"

McCook stared at Pat in disbelief, knowing, even as he did, that the scheme had merit. The IRA and Sinn Féin *had* been severely discredited, after all, both in the Catholic community at home and among their supporters in America, and that in spite of their impassioned denials of any connection with the bomber. But, even so ...

"You know you're asking me to commit vocational suicide, don't you," McCook said, trying desperately not to sound petulant, "if not to actually sign my own death warrant?"

"Yeah, well, if yeh do nothin' then the blood of all those people is on yehr hands as much as it is MacChu's. And anyway, laddie, what d'yeh want? Tunas with good taste or tunas that taste good?"

"*What*?!"

"D'yeh want to be a man of honor or to be honored just because yeh fit the description of an honorable man?"

"Why, the former, obviously, though I don't see how betraying my own people ..."

"Then think about it from the other side for minute. Would yeh want to have yehr house and yehr car and maybe yehr wife and children all burned up just because of where yeh say yehr prayers or to which crooked government yeh prefer to pay yehr taxes? If the answer to that is "No" and someone had the power to stop it, wouldn't yeh want him to use it?"

"The Golden Rule, Reverend? Really? Isn't that just a bit simplistic here?"

"It's 'Pat,' Alistair. And I don't know, so you tell me. Is it?"

McCook couldn't find an answer, dumbfounded equally, by Pat's persuasiveness and by what he knew it might make him do.

AFTER MAKING THE CALL, Hugh took off his Yankees hat and glasses, replaced them with his tweed cap and contacts and changed into a navy blue shirt. Then he cycled back to Stranraer and booked into the Royal Crescent Hotel just across the road from the ferry terminal. In his room, he fell onto the bed in deep exhaustion and didn't stir until dawn the next morning.

He awoke refreshed and smiling, happy that he'd deciphered his mother's message in time and done the right thing, and that he would now be able to make a fresh start on a new road. For all of his life up to his point, he'd let the past consume his future, had never stood back to take a look at himself and see the forlornness of all those nights spent sleeping in a chair like his father, at how hollow and meaningless his existence really was. As the stood by the window and watched the sun peep over the low eastern hills, he shook his head, grinned ruefully and asked himself aloud, "What was I thinking?"

In the shower, he contemplated his next move—to continue on to Australia per his original plan, and lay low for a while. Of course, even though he hadn't killed anyone, he would still be a very much-wanted man and, because he left clues behind, would have to be extra cautious. Still, he felt confident that there was nothing to tie him to either Hugh O'Conor or to the man he would now become. Then, when he felt safe enough in his new identity, he would return to Stranraer to find Maggie and, if she were not spoken for, to hopefully spend the rest of his life being a husband to her and a father to Toni. The thought made him smile again and feel blessed to have a second chance at happiness in life.

His mother's smiling image came to him then, and he said,

"Thank you, Mommy. Thank you for saving me."

"That's Mommy's good little boy," she replied, and Hugh wept for joy.

After dressing, he picked up his repacked duffel and started for the door. But catching sight of the small television on the dresser, he stopped, as it occurred to him that he hadn't watched a TV since before coming to Belfast. Thinking it would be a good idea to "gather intelligence" before heading into a hostile world, he switched it on.

But what Hugh saw on the screen, however, made him drop both his duffel and his jaw.

"WILL WE SEE MR. NO-NAME, Mummy?" Toni asked, as Maggie drove them through the early morning mist toward Stranraer.

"I don't think so, Toni dear. At least, not until the wind changes."

"When will that be?"

"Oh, I don't know. Maybe tomorrow."

"But Gramma Jeanne says tomorrow is always coming but never arrives."

"Aye," Maggie said with a knowing nod. "Gramma Jeanne *would* say a thing like that, now wouldn't she?"

"Aye, she would," Toni agreed, musingly imitating her mother's wisdom. "I hope the wind changes soon. I like Mr. No-name."

"Aye, Toni dear, but practically perfect people never permit sentiment to muddle their thinking, you know."

Still, she held her breath as they topped the rise, because the wind was capricious, and one just never knew what it might blow in ...

DETECTIVE SERGEANT PETER PATRICK PERKINS was a unique character among the members of the RUC, not only for his prosaically alliterative name, but also because he was the product of a mixed marriage, with his mother hailing from a Nationalist family rooted in Catholic Glencolin in the west end of West Belfast and his father from a Methodist family entrenched in Protestant Dundonald in the east end of East Belfast. The manner of their meeting was a romance novel penned by Mel Brooks and made them famous throughout the readership of the "Local News" sections of the Belfast newspapers—for exactly their fifteen Warhol-allotted minutes—as the symbols of 'peace and cross-community cooperation' in the newly-media-proclaimed "New Ulster" (which, as it turned out, was a non-starter and no different than the old one, anyway).

Both were on their noon break from their jobs on Donegall Square in the sectarian-neutral City Centre—she as a librarian at the Linenhall Library and he as a clerk at City Hall—and just happened to be passing each other on the street when a car backfired and he—lately returned from a combat tour in Korea with the Royal Ulster Rifles—heard it as an exploding mortar round, shouted "*Incoming!*" and pulled her protectively to the ground. Instantly realizing his gaffe, he leapt to his feet with a profuse and heartfelt apology on his lips, only to find her unconscious from having smacked her head on the sidewalk. Sweeping her into his arms, he took off toward Belfast City Hospital shouting "Taxi! Taxi!" as he ran, completely oblivious in his momentary dysphoria to the fact that, like cops, hookers and pubs were wont to be, there were never any taxies handy when one *really* needed them. Down Bedford Street, onto Dublin Road and all the way to Lisburn Road he ran still carrying her, before finding a taxi to take them the last mile to the hospital. Upon reaching it, however, he realized he had no money to pay the pittance of a fare, and, in a moment of severe cognitive dysfunction, grabbed her purse to see if she had any, only to have her awaken just as his hand disappeared into it.

"Here you, what're yeh after?" she exclaimed, snatching it from him.

"Oh, I ... I'm frightfully sorry. It's just that I don't seem to have any money for the fare."

"The *fare*? *What* fare? And where am I? And who are *you*?" she snapped at the gawking driver.

"He's the taxi driver," Perkins replied. "I was taking ..."

"The taxi? I didn't call for any taxi!"

"No, I ... That is, I ... I...

"He was taking you to the hospital, missus ..." the obliging driver began to explain.

"The *hospital*! I'm not *pregnant*!"

"No one said yeh were, missus."

"And I'm not *married* either!"

"Yes, missus ... I mean *miss*. Whatever you say, miss," the driver said, wisely turning his face forward and giving up the field.

"If you'll just let me explain ..." Perkins tried again.

"Sure, and be quick with yerhself, too, before I call the peelers on the both o' yez!"

"Yes, well, you see, we were passing each other on the Square when I heard what I thought was ... That is, I heard a car ... I mean, I ... I ... Y-y-you ... You tripped and knocked yourself unconscious on the sidewalk and I thought I'd better bring you to the hospital to be sure you're alright. But, when we got here I realized I didn't have any money—I was en route to my bank to cash a cheque when it happened, you see—so I ... That is, I ... I thought you might have some and that's why I ... why I ... Oh, I've made a terrible mess of this, haven't I?"

"Now, let me get this straight," she said, trying to add up his discordant facts into a harmonious sum. "I fell and hit my head ..."

"Ah, well, there *was* a bit more to it than that," he confessed, and rapidly filled her in on Korea and the rest.

"So," she deduced, "thinkin', as yeh were, that I was in danger, yeh knocked me down to save me from it. But then, when yeh saw yehr mistake and me dozin' like a wee one, yeh grabbed me up and stuffed me into this taxi and ..."

"Actually, miss, he hailed me at the corner of Bradbury and Lisburn," the driver interjected. "He carried yeh in his two arms from the Square."

"You *carried* me ...?" she asked, with a tear springing to her eye, with the rest being, as they say, *history*.

Figuring him to be the closest thing to a knight in shining armor she was likely to find, she snatched him up while the snatching was good and went from being Miss Sharon Curran to Mrs. William Perkins in barely six months time—which wasn't nearly long enough for either of their families to digest the fact of a quisling in their midst and that they'd either have to reconcile themselves to it or turn their backs on a loved one. Fortunately, while both were staunch in their beliefs, neither were fanatical enough to do the latter.

Still, the wedding was a stiff, uncomfortable affair, with the white-draped aisle demarcating the rift between "Friend of the bride?" versus "Friend of the groom?", Orange vs. Green, Catholic vs. Protestant and all of the other imaginary lines dividing their two cultural traditions. But being sublimely happy and desperately in love as they were, Sharon and William paid not the slightest attention to anything but each other. In fact, their only acknowledgment of their deeply-divided audience was that each walked down the side of the aisle adjacent to the other's family, an in-your-face gesture that said, "We're getting married, so grow up and deal with it!"

The ceremony was performed in a small non-denominational chapel just inside the Republic by a Church of Ireland minister, although, in the spirit of compromise—a thing of which their marriage would require more than its share—it was agreed that they should live halfway between Dundonald and Glencolin (or 'Solemn and Begorrah,' as they came to call them) in the harmoniously-mixed neighborhood of Ballynafeigh, and raise their children in the Church of Ireland, which William characterized to his family as being "still Protestant" and Sharon to hers as "Catholic without the Pope," which, of course, being the good compromise it was, left neither faction happy!

Once the vows were said, the rings exchanged, the bride kissed and the couple processioning back up the aisle, the two fathers came unavoidably face-to-face as they exited their pews and stood there regarding each other, two stern, steadfast and clannish men in what could potentially have been an inflammatory moment.

"Well, Mr. Perkins, they're married so," Himself of the Bride ruminated at last.

"Aye, Mr. Curran, they are indeed," rumbled Himself of the Groom.

"And there's nothin' we can do about it now."

"Nae, not a thing."

"And 'tis happy they are, wouldn't yeh say?"

"Aye, that I would."

"Then far be it for us to come a'tween them."

"Aye, far be it."

"So then, Mr. Perkins. Will we have a shake on it?"

"We will, Mr. Curran, aye."

As they shook hands then in the center of their two families, tribes and traditions, tears started in their eyes as their animosity melted into happiness for their children and they embraced heartily, each apologizing for their past transgressions against the other's ilk. Taking their cue from the patriarchs, the families streamed across the aisle to introduce themselves and embrace their new relations, mixing both in the center and on either side as the love of Sharon and William brought them together and solved, at least in a microcosm, that "awful color problem of the Orange and the Green," as the song has it.

Thereafter, the two families became voices of moderation in their respective communities and came together for holidays on the neutral ground of Sharon and William's home, to the purchase and support of which they even contributed so there would be a venue large enough to accommodate their gatherings. At first, the house was much too spacious for the newlywed's daily living, though Sharon remedied that by remaining a good Catholic in at least the practice of eschewing the family planning devices that she scornfully called "raincoats" and bearing five children in seven years, before finally agreeing with William that, for the sake of their existing children, perhaps their passion had best incorporate an interstice of lamb's gut.

Their eldest child and son, (born exactly nine months and a day after their wedding, which prompted William to bring Sharon roses with a note reading, "Thanks for making an honest man of me!"), they christened Peter Patrick, not for the saints, mind you, but for his not-so-saintly but all-things-considered-not-so-bad-either grandfathers Perkins and Curran, respectively. As "Peter," he went through the first few years of life relatively unscathed by the playground Alphas and their penchant for calling names that "will never hurt me," although, near the end of Primary 3, a young wag did tag him with "Pee-Pee" for the initials of his Christian and surname. But it was in Primary 4, however, that a particularly vicious bit of doggerel became attached to him when a Protestant schoolmate from a hard-line family learned of his mother's past Catholicism and of his middle name, "Patrick," and incorporated them and the more lascivious meaning of his first name into:

"Peter's a peter 'n so's 'is daddy!
His mudder's a Taig an' he's a Paddy!"

It's impetus petered out rather quickly, however, because Peter's growing prowess as a forward on his school's football team—and his mates' fraternal protectiveness—soon insulated him from the more malicious genre of teasing, as well as the baser sort of people who perpetrated it.

Not that it had bothered him in the least, anyway, as he just let it roll off his back with a patient sort of not-quite-patronizing smile, almost as if to say "Is that really the best you can do?" For Peter Patrick Perkins was born of Grace in the form of his parents' healing love, and, from an early age, he was possessed of a contemplative equanimity and quiet confidence that made him a sure thinker and a steadying influence on his family, friends and peers, as well as a natural-born intermediary, a gift he called upon many times as he grew to manhood amid the endemic communal strife of Northern Ireland.

Upon his graduation from secondary school, rather than acceding to his parents' wishes and going on to university, Peter followed his father's footsteps into the army regiment known as the Royal Irish Rangers, where he rose through the enlisted ranks as easily and naturally as if being pulled from above by a godly force. Upon completing his enlistment, he again shunned academia and enlisted in the Royal Ulster Constabulary because, as he told his father, "I've a knack for bringin' people together and I want to use it to help end The Troubles, and that'll never happen unless people can begin to see the issues from the other side. And, since I'm the closest thing to a Catholic the RUC will ever accept, I figure it's my duty to join."

"But why put your life on the line like that?" his father countered. "Couldn't you serve better by continuing your education and becoming a solicitor or a social-worker, or even a politician or minister, God forbid?"

"Oh, Da," Peter shrugged with a rueful grin. "You know I'm not uppity like that. I just want to get my hands on it and go to work."

Hearing that, his father could only grin himself and concede, for he knew his son very well—and knew that Peter did, too.

Although he'd picked up the handle of "Peep" in the army, it was during his Constabulary training that Peter acquired the epithet that would stick to him for all his remaining days, when, barely a nanosecond after the screen debut of the iconic Lucasfilm character C-3-P-O, one of his quicker classmates dubbed him "Three-Pee-O'Perkins." With the raging popularity of *Star Wars*, it traveled quickly and he was soon known as 3-P-O throughout the *Force* and beyond. Not only did Peter accept it with his customary good nature, but, with his own wry sense of humor and appreciation for the sardonic subtlety and mischievous causticity of the Irish wit, he embraced it as particularly apt, although not due to the obvious elements of the Three Pees and his Catholic mother, but because his namesake was a "protocol droid" who served as an intermediary between disparate cultures, just as Peter felt it was his calling to do. Aside from that, being known as 3-P-O gave him a certain air of cool, a Hollywood cachet, almost, especially among younger people, which helped disarm the innate and instantaneous hostility he often encountered in his work, especially in Nationalist neighborhoods. That, in turn, opened the door to him telling of his mixed parentage and, thereby, laying a foundation for rapport with the citizenry, whom he found to be mostly decent and genuinely willing to accept an excuse to put aside their fears and prejudices and follow the brighter angels of their nature. In that rather obvious though paradoxically under-recognized manner, he came to be—if not exactly welcomed—at least trusted to be fair and forthright by both communities.

It was this ability to get "Just the facts, ma'am," from both sides of the divide that brought the dedicated but work-a-day Constable Perkins to the attention of the ambitious Detective-Inspector McCook, who was busily chewing through cases, honing his executive and organizational skills and going to night school for a combined law and business-management degree, and desperately needed a capable assistant to take over his investigative and other more-administrative duties. And while it might've seemed like an "Odd-Couple" combination for the incongruous nature of their career and personal objectives as policemen, their minds and skill-sets worked in complement and allowed each to further his own ambitions. For Perkins, who lived simply and found no intrinsic value in climbing the rank or salary ladders, being promoted on McCook's coattails afforded a higher profile from which to do his community relations work as well as more "extra" cash to donate to his favored charities. It also allowed McCook—who hated doing the flatfoot work anyway, especially when it involved Nationalists, who were, by the nature of their de facto second-class citizenship, inherently obstructionist—to play to his strength, which was his innate ability to consider the pieces of a case as if they were a jigsaw puzzle and assemble them into a logical, deductive whole, as well as "leisure" time to cultivate relationships among his superiors and cohorts in other services, all of which, in the long view of things, made him a better policeman and facilitated his rapid rise to Detective-Superintendent.

So it was in this way that Perkins had risen to Detective-Inspector himself—even though many on the force took a dim view of his "Paddy-pandering," as they called it—and had a staff of men and women working for him who were like-minded in their approach to The Troubles. And it was in this way, too, that he came to shake hands with Reverend Pat MacDonnell across the sketch-artist's drawing board, a meeting of two men who wanted to help people brought randomly together from polar opposite beginnings—one each from the worst and the best that the people of Northern Ireland had within them—and a chance encounter on a late-night ferry.

"Superintendent McCook asked me to fetch you on my way in," Perkins said. "That is, if you're done here?"

"Aye, we're just boxin' it up so," Pat replied. Looking at the sketch, he continued, "That's yehr man, MacChu, so he is, unless I'm much mistaken."

"Doesn't look much like the description we have from the neighborhood, except around the eyes and nose, maybe. Have you seen the sketch we put in the papers?"

"Aye, laddie, I have, and I know where yeh're goin' with that. Yeh're thinkin' that maybe it corrupted me memory, and, sure, that's always possible. But, just so yeh know, I was a Garda in me youth and I've never broken the habit of measurin' people for their particulars. So I think I can say with a good amount of certainty that the resemblance is authentic and not induced."

Perkins considered that for a moment, giving Pat a second look. That he'd been a policeman himself lent credence to his story, of course, but more so, the fact that he spoke intelligently and logically, if with something of a South Armagh culchie accent. Though there were questions he wanted to ask, he also knew his boss was waiting.

Turning to the sketch artist, he said, "Please get a copy of that to Superintendent McCook's office as soon as you can." Then he motioned for Pat to precede him. "Reverend MacDonnell, if you please?"

"Just plain Pat will do, laddie. And I'll follow you."

When they reached McCook's office, they found him sitting at his desk staring at the blanket of files and notes that smothered it, the distant, fearsome look in his eyes telling Perkins that he was deep in thought trying to assemble the pieces of his case into some sort of operable structure. Knowing better than to interrupt, he motioned Pat to a chair and took one himself, where they waited silently to be acknowledged.

"What do you have for me, 3-P-O?" McCook said finally, drawing his eyes and mind slowly back to the people in front of him.

"Not much, chief." Perkins replied. "We've turned the place upside down and back again and found nothing that adds to what we already know. My people are re-canvassing the neighborhood, too, but I doubt they'll come across anything. Our man just knows how to cover his tracks."

McCook grunted. "You might say that."

"I've had a thought on the fingerprints, though. It seems to me that ..."

"Fingerprints! That's it!" McCook interrupted, snapping his fingers. "That's what I was trying to remember. I read somewhere once that a suspect couldn't be fingerprinted because he didn't have any. When they asked what happened to them, he said he'd never had any, that he was born without them! So if MacChu were born without fingerprints and joined an intelligence service or special forces, like Pat thinks, then they'd have a record of it!

"Janice!" McCook shouted, banging at the buttons on his intercom. "*Janice!*"

"Yes, chief?"

"Get Dan Sullivan with CIA on the phone! Tell him it's an emergency!"

"Yes, chief."

"The Yanks, chief?" Perkins asked.

"Fill him in, Pat!" McCook ordered, rising from his chair to pace the room furiously. "And consider yourself deputized until I tell you otherwise. I need all the good minds working on this I can get!"

"Thanks for that," Pat said, appreciating the complement, before realizing that McCook had also effectively *interned* him for as long as he wanted. "Or at least I think so, anyway."

As Pat spoke to Perkins, Janice's voice came over the intercom. "Dan Sullivan on the line, chief."

Without a reply, McCook snatched up the phone. "Hello, Dan. I think we might have a lead on our man and I need your help to track it down." He paused then to listen. "Grand. That's grand, indeed, and thank you. We think he's Irish-American, has Special Forces or Intelligence training and was possibly born without identifiable fingerprints. It's that last bit that's the kicker. If you ever had someone with that trait in your camp, it would be in his file, wouldn't it?" He paused to listen. "Yes, Dan, I know. But I don't have time to go through that right now. If you could just run a check based on that piece of info, it would be grand." He paused to listen. "Sure, alright. Thanks, Dan. I'll owe you large for this one." He paused to listen. "Yes, and to yours."

"Well, what do you think?" McCook asked Perkins when Pat finished his briefing.

"Sounds like a stretch to me, chief. On the other hand, it might just be a rather brilliant bit of police work by our Pat here. It depends on what the Americans come up with."

"Yes, it does, doesn't it? And here, he thought having no fingerprints would cover his tracks when it's going to lead us right to him."

"Actually," Pat countered, "I think he thought it didn't matter because he was goin' to incinerate the evidence, anyway. It's the changin' of his mind that's doin' him in so."

"Yes, good point. And it seems that we have you to thank for that," McCook said.

"Oh, now, don't start down that road with me. As I said, all I did was give him somethin' to think about. He changed his own mind. And yeh have to credit him that much, at least."

"I'll credit him with my hands on his throat, if it's all the same to you. And weren't you the one talking about the innocent lives being lost? Those are on his hands *first*, you know."

"If this American is indeed our man, that is," Perkins interjected, sensing tension developing and deftly reminding them that the cart was in danger of preceding the horse.

"Right yeh are, Inspector," Pat agreed. "And Superintendent, since yeh won't know that till we hear from the Yanks, hadn't yeh better get on with protectin' those lives like we talked about?"

Seeing the look that passed between Pat and McCook then, Perkins said, "Is there something I should know, chief?"

McCook sighed and flicked a hand at Pat. "Go ahead. Fill him in."

Turning to Perkins, Pat explained his idea for quelling the sectarian violence by neutralizing the Protestant paramilitaries.

"Sure, that's *desperate!*" Perkins said at the end, looking rather frightened. "Are we going to do it, chief? Don't get me wrong. I think it's a workable scheme, but it would surely be the end of us all with the Constabulary. I don't care so much about me, but most of my people have families and can't afford to lose their jobs."

"Do you think I don't know that?" McCook shot back. "Hell, I'd probably have go live in Arizona with the Mafia just to save my own skin. But do you have any better ideas? You're the one who wants to bring justice to Ulster for all her people."

Having nothing to say, Perkins said exactly that.

"Yes, that's what I thought," McCook said. "But maybe we won't have to do it if the Americans come up with something. We can release the sketch or maybe even a photo to the press and put out the word that he's a lone wolf, a madman who isn't even Irish, much less IRA. Then we can release the Provos, except for the ones we want anyway, and lean on the UDA and UVF to call off their dogs without having to arrest the leaders."

"Sure, that'll be nice for you and everything will have a happy endin', tra-la-la," Pat objected. "But what if they don't come up with anything? Or what if they do but it takes several days? Who's goin' to protect the Catholics in the interim?"

McCook glared at Pat and, for a moment, Perkins feared that his chief might do something rash. But then McCook sighed again. "Their computers are pretty fast and if they have anything it won't take them long to find it. With the five-hour time difference, we'll give them till midnight here to come up with something. In the interim, 3-P-O, you put together a plan for rounding up the leaders. It'll be volunteers only and you'll need to pull them in all at once to avoid any tip-offs. And Pat, you sit right there and come up with a *better* idea! Any questions?"

"Yeah, actually," Pat said with a grin. "Why do you call yehr man *3-P-O*?"

"Oh, don't ask," McCook replied.

WHEN HUGH WAS IN HIGH SCHOOL, he'd read one of Hemingway's Nick Adams stories called *The Killers*. It was spare and stark in the way that only "Papa" could render those adjectives, and concerned a former prizefighter who'd crossed some hard men and knew they were coming for him, coming to kill him, but lacked the will to do anything about it, even when Nick tried to prod him. He'd given up on life and just lay on his bed in his rented room, fully dressed and waiting for the courage to come to take the last action necessary to actually *give up* his life, to go out on the street where the assassins could find him.

As Hugh lay on the bed staring at the ceiling in his own rented room, he understood how the prizefighter felt, for although he'd been lying there for two days and knew his own life was over, he still found the final action difficult to take.

So much had changed so suddenly, and he'd gone from the high of completing his quest to the low of seeing it undone to the exhilaration of getting a second chance at life to the deflation and depression that came with those video images on TV—street battles amid burning houses captioned by BELFAST IN FLAMES. AT LEAST 80 DEAD, HUNDREDS INJURED IN ATTACKS, RIOTING. It was not something he'd anticipated, although he now felt foolish for not. He thought he could just stop the detonation and that would be the end of it, more or less, that he could take up another disguise, spirit himself away and start over. Instead, he'd thrown gasoline on the fire and now the hatred and divisions would be more entrenched than ever, the opposite of what he'd intended.

On top of that, the authorities knew who he was and had launched an intensive manhunt, with his old CIA photograph and current description blaring from every news outlet in the world. With all that in the wind, he couldn't escape now even if he wanted to, not without plastic surgery, anyway.

So it was a good thing he didn't want to.

PAT WAS STILL CLOISTERED WITH MCCOOK in the early evening when Janice's voice came over the intercom. "Sir, it's Dan Sullivan."

"Yes, Dan?" McCook fairly shouted as he snatched the receiver to his ear. As he listened, a grin split his face and he bounced in his chair like a boy who had to pee. "Excellent! *Excellent*! Give me the highlights," he said, scribbling notes as he listened. "That's *fantastic*, Dan! Thank you! Thank you! From the bottom of my heart, a thousand times, *thank you*!"

He was already in motion when he tossed down the receiver and said to Pat, "Come on."

Just beyond the door they were met by a constable running toward them with a full-page color photograph fresh from the laser printer. Without slowing his pace, McCook grabbed it and passed it to Pat.

"That's him!" Pat said. "Or at least it's a young-fellah version of him."

McCook grabbed it back as he barged into a conference room where Perkins was closeted with some of his staff. Handing him the photo, McCook exclaimed, "We've *got* him, Perkins, we've got the bastard, we've *got* him!"

"Sir?" Perkins asked.

"That's him there and Pat confirmed it. He's American. His name is Hugh O'Conor. He jumped to CIA from Special Forces and was one of their rising stars. His father owned a small foundry business near Tucson, Arizona, but his mother was an heiress. His IQ is in the stratosphere and he has a degree in Metallurgy from MIT and a PhD in Nuclear Physics from the University of Chicago. Got it when he was only twenty-three years old! And get this—he was killed in a covert operation against the Soviets in Afghanistan. Burned and mutilated beyond recognition. Not that it mattered, because he was only identified by witnesses who saw him die from a *distance*! It's the perfect cover!

"And one more thing." McCook paused for dramatic effect. "His father died suddenly when he was fifteen, but his mother and little sister were killed in the Talbot Street bombing in Dublin back in '74. You know what that means don't you, Perkins?"

"It means it was personal to him and not political," Pat interjected. "Would his mother and sister be Bridget and Maeve O'Conor then?"

McCook consulted the info sheet that came with the photo. "Why, yes, they were. How did you know?"

"I used to walk by the memorial when I was a beat cop. I didn't memorize 'em on purpose, but I read the names so many times over that they just stuck."

But McCook wasn't listening anymore. Dublin was out of his jurisdiction, 1974 was ancient history and his mind was consumed with the boost this success would give his career.

"Can you believe it, Perkins?!" he exclaimed, fairly dancing with glee. "He's a fucking *genius* with CIA training, his own money and the perfect cover, and we got him anyway!"

"Well, actually, chief, we don't have him yet," Perkins pointed out, almost shouting over the excitement in the room.

"Right!" McCook agreed, pulling himself suddenly and immediately back into business mode. "Quiet everyone! *Quiet*! Perkins, are these the volunteers?"

"Yes, chief."

"You men can be stand down for now, but stay in this room until further notice. Understood?"

"Yes, chief," came the chorused answer.

Pointing at one of the constables, McCook said, "Cameron, you come with us." Nodding at the door, he said, "Perkins. Pat."

After leading them back into his office, McCook closed the door and turned to Pat. "Reverend, you are now the most important person in the British Isles because you're the only one who can identify O'Conor on sight. I'm sorry to have to do this to you, but, as of this moment, you're confined to this room and no calls allowed.

"Cameron, take up station outside my door. If Reverend MacDonnell needs the jacks, you go with him, straight there, straight back and guard him with your life! Understood?"

"Yes, chief."

"This is hardly necessary, Alistair," Pat protested. "I'm happy to cooperate of me own accord."

"As I said, Pat, I'm sorry, but I'm taking no chances."

"Can't I at least notify my church?"

"I'll have Janice do it. Write down the number and contact."

Turning then to Perkins, he said, "3-P-O. Get the photo and sketch into the media immediately. We need this on every telly in Britain and Éire within the hour and worldwide as soon as possible. Also, post the dedicated phone line in the conference room as the contact and detail your volunteers to man it. We can move it to the communications center later, but that'll do for now."

"Yes, chief, I'm on it."

To Pat, McCook said, "I'll have Janice order in. You like Chinese?"

IT WAS A COMFORTABLE and comforting evening ritual the Galbraiths had, after supper was eaten and the dishes collaboratively washed and stowed away, to puddle into their old-but-comfortably-familiar overstuffed sofa and watch the evening news and a favorite program or two on telly, her father stretched across from the far end with his big feet almost at her hip and Maggie upright on the other end with Toni's curly, sweet-smelling head cuddled beneath her chin. There Toni would precede her Grampa into slumber-land, she sleeping sound and quiet in her mother's arms while Graham often woke himself with his snoring and sputtering, only to doze off again and repeat the cycle. Maggie would just smile and feel the warmth welling up inside her as she hoped beyond hoping for the moment to never end. "The best part of the day," she called it in her mind, her own private name for those minutes spent basking in the love of her little family and her own cherishing of them.

But on this particular evening it was Maggie who slipped away first, being exhausted from her unusually-grueling day and the fact that she'd slept poorly the night before, having awoken from dreams of a sinister white-haired stranger breaking into her house and her defenses all failing to stave him off. Just as he wrapped his hands around her throat, she thrashed herself awake and lay in the deep darkness of her room gasping for air, as if she'd been choked in reality.

What did it mean, she wondered, relating the white-haired man to the stranger on the road? Was he coming for her? Was the dream warning her of danger, shaking a finger in her face and telling her she'd been too friendly with him, that she'd given away too much information about herself and Toni? But surely not. Not *that* man, anyway. He was so shy and gentle and kind, and his face lit up when he smiled and he'd been so touched by the beauty of Toni and so appreciative, so ... reverent almost of the beauty he found in Maggie, herself. Surely someone like that would never harm her, or even intend such a thing. So it was only a dream then, a dream carrying the message that she should be more aware of her own safety and of Toni's, and the stranger, Mr. No-name ... *Hugh* ... was only in it because of the way they'd met. Yes, that was it. Just a dream telling her to be more careful.

Still the fear was slow to leave and she lay awake until the black of night began to bleed into the charcoal of dawn, while the depressive fatigue of post-trauma weighed upon her during the day.

So when Toni's excited voice broke into her sleep with, "Look, Mummy, it's Mr. No-name! Mr. No-name is on telly!" she jerked roughly upright on the sofa.

"What? What did you say?" she asked, trying to clear her mind.

"Shh! Quiet!" her father said, and she looked over to find him upright and leaning intently forward.

Following his eyes to the telly she saw that Hugh was indeed there, or at least a good rendering of him in artist's pencil, complete with the glasses and baseball cap pulled low over his eyes. Next to that was a photo of what looked like him in a younger man's skin, though his close-cropped hair was black and he stared out at the world stern and unsmiling, like in a license photo or mug shot, or like in her dream of the night before. At the bottom of the screen in bold block letters she read the name "Hugh O'Conor" and beneath it the phrase "Wanted for Questioning" and a telephone number in Belfast. Then the announcer's voice broke into her consciousness.

"... should be considered armed and extremely dangerous. If you see him do not, repeat, do *not* approach him, but call your local police at once!"

105

"Is that him, Maggie?" her father asked, pointing a shaking finger at the telly. "Is that the man who changed your tyre, the one you almost ran down in the road?"

PAT AND MCCOOK were still sitting at the desk, the detritus of their meal between them, when Perkins came running in from the conference room.

"Chief, we've got a woman over in Portpatrick who claims to have seen O'Conor. Described him to a tee. Says she almost ran him down in her car. The time she gave was less than an hour before he called in the threat. Says he's an American and was cycling toward her on the wrong side of the road coming over a rise and she missed him by inches. Says she got a puncture from running on the shoulder and he changed it for her. Can you believe that, chief, *he changed her tyre*?!"

"Is she credible?"

"As far as I can tell, although she sounded rather shaken."

"Alright, good. They're on alert over in Scotland, so have them scramble the SAS to guard her house. Nobody in or out till we get there. Janice! Janice, *damn it*, where are you?"

"Yes, chief?" she called through the open door.

"Have them warm up the chopper! Perkins and I are off to Portpatrick!

"You, too, Pat," McCook continued, as he grabbed a briefcase and began stuffing it.

But Pat sat unmoving, rooted to the spot by the thought stuck in his mind. "Superintendent?" he said softly.

"Yes, Pat, what?" McCook asked, still moving feverishly.

"Yeh do realize, don't yeh, that with the failsafe timer, if that woman had hit O'Conor, both you and Belfast would be a pile o' smoulderin' ash now?"

That stopped McCook cold for a moment and he stood blinking at Pat. Then he smiled.

"Yes, but she *didn't* hit him, now *did* she?"

AFTER MAGGIE PLACED THE CALL to Belfast, it didn't take long for things to get interesting. First, their local police showed up to place a cordon around their house and order them to stay inside. Then there were endless sirens and flashing lights as more and more police arrived from further afield to set up roadblocks and order everyone off the streets upon the pain of incarceration and worse! But the *coup de grace* came when the Special Air Service swooped in and made a circus of roping into their yard from helicopters, before establishing an armed perimeter that included enough firepower to handily erase their house and everything in it. It was like something out of a Hollywood film, and they didn't know whether to be frightened or just break out the popcorn.

Soon, however, they heard the "whup-whup-whup" of another chopper and Maggie watched from the window as it landed in the field adjacent to their house amid flares set out to mark a landing zone. Three men alit and were guided toward the house by two heavily-armed soldiers.

"There's some men coming to the door, Daddy," Maggie said, and Graham opened it and beckoned them inside.

The first one in held up his identification card and said politely but firmly. "Graham Galbraith? I'm Detective-Superintendent Alistair McCook of the Royal Ulster Constabulary, and this ..."

But before he could continue his introductions, Toni sat bolt upright in her mother's lap and in her best Muppet voice said, "Dis Monsterpiece Theatre. Me Alistair Cookie."

At that, the queerest sort of look crossed McCook's suddenly-crimson face—an unmelodious mélange of astonishment, horror and withering glare—and his jaw dangled as if he'd been struck dumb. At that, the man next to him had to stifle a laugh while the third, who was taller and older than the other two, just looked bewildered.

"Did I miss somethin'?" the latter asked with a heavy brogue.

"Oh, don't ask," the second snickered.

"Sure, 3-P-O, but I've been hearin' that a lot lately," said the older man, which sent the second into an affected paroxysm of coughing to cover the fact that he was roaring with laughter.

"Are you quite finished, Perkins?" McCook asked tersely, turning an icy glower on him.

"Yes, chief," Perkins replied, pulling himself together with a saga-worthy effort. "Sorry, chief."

McCook turned back to them then, but before he could say anything, Graham growled, "Cookie Monster? C-3-P-O? What is this? The Keystone Kops?"

At that, Perkins could no longer contain himself and bolted unceremoniously from the house.

McCook just sighed, closed his eyes and shook his head. "Do you mind if I sit down?" he asked Graham

"Nae, I think you'd better!" Graham replied. "And you, too, Officer ...?

"Reverend, actually," the third man said, reaching across to shake hands. "Ian Patrick MacDonnell. But you can just call me plain Pat."

"Reverend, is it?" Graham turned back to McCook. "You Irish always pack a Druid when you invade another country?"

McCook smiled weakly. "Can I go out and start over?"

"Nae, laddie," Graham chuckled. "I think it's a bit late for first impressions. But look. I'm not sure exactly what happened here, but I know you gentlemen are serious about getting this madman off the street and anything we can do to help, you have but to ask."

"Thank you, Mr. Galbraith," McCook replied. "Pat, will you please corral Perkins and bring him inside?"

Once they were all together and settled into chairs, the men got down to business, giving Maggie a thorough but courteous interrogation—even taking Toni's interjections seriously. Then Pat shared his story of meeting Hugh O'Conor on the ferry and he and Maggie compared notes to be certain they were speaking of the same man. When all the questions were asked and it was established that Maggie had last seen O'Conor on the morning of the call and knew nothing of his further movements, McCook and company rose to leave.

But at the door, Pat turned to Maggie and said, "You do realize, don't you, that if you'd hit him, Belfast would be in ruins now?"

The thought of it made Maggie dizzy and she flopped onto the sofa as if pushed. "Nae, I hadn't thought of it. It's a good thing Daddy taught me to drive so well."

Pat smiled and winked at Graham then, saying, "Good man, yehrself!"

THOUGH THE DAY WAS GRAY with low-hanging clouds, Hugh squinted as he sat on the park bench looking at the harbor of Stranraer, for he hadn't set foot out of his room in days and the light glinting on the water smarted his red and crusty eyes. He was thin and weak, too, and though stiff and sore from lying on the bed so long, exhausted from infrequent and shallow sleep, and with his new growth of heavy white beard, he looked twenty years older than his age.

With his rage gone and knowing now that any sort of future life was just a delusion, Hugh had nothing left to sustain himself. He knew he'd wasted his life and squandered the gifts he'd been given. He knew, too, that he was guilty and would be punished for his sins, even as he was already punishing himself by withholding food and taking water only because he had to live long enough to emulate Emmet and make a speech from the dock, to apologize for creating further troubles in Northern Ireland and tell them that there was only one important sentence in all of creation—"Do unto others as you would have them do unto you." If he could just do that, then maybe it wouldn't have *all* been a waste.

Then his gut twisted with hunger and he wondered aloud, "Ah, Jesus, why haven't they come for me yet?"

AFTER THREE DAYS of fruitless searching for O'Conor, the authorities concluded that he'd fled the area, lifted the curfew and moved on, leaving every single person in Portpatrick to pour into the pubs simultaneously. Naturally, the Galbraiths were the topic of discussion and Graham's local was packed to the rafters and out the door with people hoping he'd make an appearance and tell their story. But they all went home disappointed, if a bit more than usually inebriated, because Maggie and Graham wisely chose to sequester themselves behind closed doors and drawn shades.

So it wasn't till the following day that Maggie ventured forth in her car to pick up some things from school and run errands in Stranraer. Finished and on her way home, she was driving by the small park that fronted the harbor when she caught a glimpse of a white-haired man sitting on a bench. Thinking that it was O'Conor but needing a better look, she braked quickly and took a screeching right onto the street bounding the park, causing the driver behind her to lay on his horn in protest.

Realizing that the commotion might've attracted the man's attention, she pulled her car behind a boundary hedge and waited for her heart to stop pounding with fear. Thinking suddenly that he might have recognized her and could be coming for her at that very moment made her gasp and look wildly around as she locked her doors. But he was nowhere in sight and, anyway, if he were really afraid of being seen, why would he sit there in full view of passers-by, as if waiting for someone to come and get him?

Feeling somewhat reassured, Maggie got out of her car and peeked over the hedge, though all she could see was the back of the man's head. Trying for a better angle, she moved along the hedge, but came to its end without improving her view. Taking a deep breath, she stepped into the open, only to watch him turn toward her.

"Hello, Maggie," Hugh said calmly. "I thought that was you driving dangerously. I hope Toni isn't with you."

But Maggie couldn't answer, only gape at the shadow of a man who sat before her, listless, hollow-eyed, almost lifeless. "What's happened to you, Hugh?" she managed at last. "You look awful!"

"It's interesting you should say so," Hugh replied, looking at her intently, "since this is the first time I've felt truly human since I was eight years old." Then he smiled, sadly but very gently, and Maggie was no longer afraid *of* him but afraid *for* him.

Fighting away sudden panic, she asked, "Why are you sitting here in the open, where everyone can see you?"

"I've been waiting for someone to turn me in," he replied. "I'm glad it'll be you, since it was our meeting that convinced me not to go through with it. I have a room in the hotel just over there and they have a phone in the lobby you can use. Please go call the police and I'll just wait here."

"You ... You'll just *wait*?" Maggie stammered, stricken with the pathos of all the phrase left unsaid—"I'll just wait here *for them to come and get me, for them to treat me roughly and humiliate me before locking me away and throwing away the key*."

"Yes, I'll just wait here. I know they'll come quickly. So please make the call, Maggie. I'm ready now and I want to get it over with."

Still Maggie couldn't move because her heart ached with sorrow and the hopeless desire to turn back the clock and save this poor man from himself.

"Why did you do it, Hugh? *Why?*" she asked, wanting desperately to know, to understand, to *feel* herself what it was that had driven him to such desperate and despicable measures.

He sighed and looked away. "I don't know, Maggie. *Revenge*, I suppose. That would be the simplest answer, anyway. They killed my mother and sister, you know, and then my father died of a broken heart. I wanted revenge for what they'd done to us and perhaps I thought wrapping it up in a grand scheme to avenge all the wrongs done to Ireland would somehow justify mass murder. At least, that's the way it unfolded in the end, though I really don't remember thinking it out in those terms. I was a child when it began and I never stopped to think about what killing a hundred thousand people would really mean. It was just a number to me and had no face or name till I met you and Toni. Even that might not have mattered if I hadn't met that minister on the ferry, who told me that the battle for the human soul is fought within the human heart and it's about balancing self-interest against doing right by others. And then I had these visions of my mother telling me about the Golden Rule, and you said to me, 'How would you feel if you'd been in my place?' I saw all these faces in my head, mothers with babies and fathers with kids in the park. I put myself in their place and that's when I knew that I didn't really want to kill them, because they aren't *all* guilty, after all, especially the children."

"*Guilty*, Hugh? Guilty of what?"

"It doesn't matter," he sighed. "None of it matters now, except that I didn't go through with it in the end. And that I apologize for the evil I *have* done and try to make something positive come of it. That's the only value my life has now.

"So go make the call, Maggie. *Please*. I'll just wait here."

She hesitated for a moment, wanting desperately for there to be something more, something, *anything*. But finding nothing, she said, "Alright, Hugh, I'll ... No. No, wait. If I call they'll bring guns and someone might get hurt. *You* might get hurt. So let me take you to them. They're just a couple of streets over. That way, you can turn yourself in peacefully. Alright?"

"The police are just a couple of streets over? Well, that explains why no one has called yet. They wouldn't think of looking for me right under their noses. It's always the best place to commit a crime, you know, right in front of the station house. No one ever looks for anything right under their nose.

"But, OK. You're right. I don't want to cause any more trouble. So I'll come with you. I'll duck down in your car till we get there so no one will see me with you."

The drive to the station took less than a minute. When they arrived, Hugh said, "Thank you, Maggie, for all you've done for me."

But her heart was in her throat and she couldn't reply, just took his hand and squeezed it. He smiled again, that warm natural smile that came from his heart and showed what an asset he might've been to humanity, and Maggie's heart leapt from her throat and shattered on the ground.

Then Hugh got out of the car and she watched through tears as he walked into the station, but didn't wait for the door to close behind him.

THE REVEREND IAN PATRICK MACDONNELL sat at his breakfast table staring out the window with his eyes focused a thousand yards within himself, the cause of his abstraction being the morning paper lying atop his now-cold breakfast.

ARREST IN DOWNING OF CHOPPER
RUC ADMIN ACCUSED OF LEAK

After an intensive investigation into the explosion of the helicopter transporting suspected nuclear terrorist Hugh O'Conor from Scotland to Northern Ireland, the Royal Ulster Constabulary have arrested Janice Gilmartin of Belfast and charged her with eleven counts of murder in the second degree. Gilmartin, an RUC employee and former executive assistant to the late Detective-Superintendent Alistair McCook, is alleged to have supplied an as-yet unknown contact within the Irish Republican Army with information that led to the planting of a bomb aboard the chopper. Killed in the incident were O'Conor, McCook, Detective-Inspector Peter Perkins, two crewmen and eight soldiers.

The IRA released a statement shortly after the incident taking credit for the explosion and stating that, while they regretted the loss of life, they wanted O'Conor dead because they disapproved of his methods and wanted to send a message to anyone else who might be contemplating such a scheme.

A source within RUC who spoke on condition of anonymity said that, when questioned as to why she betrayed her boss, Gilmartin replied, "For twelve years, all he did was scream at me *'Janice do this!'* and *'Janice do that!'* with never so much as a 'please' or 'thank you' or even a pat on the back! One does tire of being treated so, you know. I mean, how would he have liked it if he'd been in my shoes?"

THE END?